THE WATCHERS AND THE GIFTED ONES

THE PANTHER TALES

DANIELLA RUSHTON
ILLUSTRATED BY ZOE POTTER

The Watchers and the Gifted Ones: The Panther Tales / Rushton- 2nd Edition

ISBN: 978-1-913795-00-9 (First Edition)

ISBN: 978-1-953610-02-7 (Second Edition)

1.Title. 2. The Watchers and the Gifted Ones. 3. Fantasy. 4. Fiction.
5. Rushton.

Cover art and interior art by Zoe Potter

First Edition Published by
For the Right Reasons
38 Grant Street
Inverness, IV3 8BN
Scotland

Second Edition Published by
NFB Publishing/Amelia Press
119 Dorchester Road
Buffalo, New York 14213

For more information visit Nfbpublishing.com

Dear Bertie,

The summer of two thousand and seventeen was extraordinarily memorable. It was the year that you travelled with your Grandparents, 'oceans away' to America.

It was also of course, the year you challenged me to write this book. In doing so you opened my heart and mind creating an imaginative world, as well as lifelong friends upon the way.

Thank you, Bertie.

Mummy x

My heartfelt thanks to Nicholas for his unfailing love and to Zoe, Michael and John, for their unwavering support.

The Watchers and The Gifted Ones

The Panther Tales

RECOMMENDED INSPIRATIONAL LISTENING, COLLATED TO REFLECT THE MOOD OF THE FOLLOWING CHAPTERS.

'LET YOUR IMAGINATION FLY'

- DANIELLA

CHAPTER 1

You & Me Flume Remix Disclosure, featuring Eliza Doolittle, 2012

A key feature of the story is how the relationship between Parky the panther and Hannah develop. From the moment she glances over and sees him for the first time, it really is all about them.

CHAPTER 3

Moving, Supergrass

The energy of the story, the trials and tribulations begin to take place. Hannah's journey is flowing, she is on the move, come what may.

CHAPTER 5

Aquarium - Carnival of the Animals Camille Saint Saëns

A house alive with oddities. A surreal walk. A mysterious meeting.

CHAPTER 7

Unforgettable, Nat King Cole, The Ultimate Collection.

Friendships engrave our being and build the tapestry of our lives.

CHAPTER 9

Bad Guy, Billie Eilish & Justin Bieber

Feathers come together, wrapped up in a coil of devastation. It's the dark side.

CHAPTER 11

No Tears Left to Cry, Ariana Grande

Dried out of not only tears but also emotion.

The rawness felt exemplifies Tom's desperation.

CHAPTER 13

Conquest of Paradise, Vangelis

Spine tingling, rousing and evoking feelings of pride.

Mission accomplished. It is done.

CHAPTER 15

For the Love of a Princess, James Horner

A love shared that will last an eternity. No greater love.

CONTENTS

CHAPTER ONE

HANNAH'S GIFT

HANNAH TIMMS walked through a pair of high, white, double vaulted doors. She was sixteen years old and the twin to Amelia, her flaming red haired sister whom she had left at home in the small market town of Ashby-by-the-Sea, England, where she had lived her entire life, in a three storey neatly proportioned townhouse with its beautiful Georgian architecture resembling a doll's house. The heavily studded black front door was the gateway to a bustling, thriving town with throngs of people, many of whom had lived and worked in the town all their lives.

Hannah couldn't recall one single day that she had ever felt alone in her hometown. From the chitter chatter and cheery exchanges that could be heard outside from behind the Georgian sash windows, to the gaiety of locals greeting in the street. Ashby-by-the-Sea was quite simply alive and a world within itself.

It was made even more special as it hosted its very own castle, only a stone's throw from the towns centre. A huge great tower formed part of its medieval ruins which hovered over the town like a prehistoric albatross. It was a feature, not only cherished but also feared by locals. For centuries, dark rumours had perpetuated and even to this day still existed about the castle.

Despite the usual busyness of her town, Hannah now found herself very much alone, as she was spending the summer at Mini's, her Grandmother.

Quite the opposite to Hannah, not only in looks but also in personality, the twins had not been getting along for some time. Amelia had become increasingly disagreeable in a way Hannah couldn't quite describe. It was much more than bickering and after much correspondence with their Grandmother, whom she had only met a few times, Hannah now found herself on the highly polished hall floor of Mini's magnificent home.

The twins' father, Timothy, who Hannah was probably most like was a scientist. He was both critical yet at the same time ambivalent about her summer vacation knowing that Mini lived 'oceans away.'

The girls squabbling was only part of the reason that Timothy and Belinda, their mother and Mini's daughter, had encouraged Hannah to go.

So now Timothy had resigned himself to watch patiently from the side-lines, whilst his beautiful blonde-haired wife quietly co-ordinated what both parents knew was an essential trip for their fair-haired daughter to Palms, America, where Mini lived; much to the annoyance of feisty Amelia.

"Absence will make their hearts grow fonder," was their father's new mantra.

Standing whilst yawning, Hannah dropped her bags, scruffily in the hallway and kicked off her old and battered pale blue trainers. Feeling slightly dazed she stood looking around. It had been quite a journey to Palms which was a desert-like place surrounded by naked mountains, filled with lofty palm trees and neatly placed neighbourhoods of all kinds dotted here and there. Hannah was tired, hungry and now tired again.

The black and white diamond floor tiles in the hallway resembled a giant checkerboard and to the left there was a large, wooden, sweeping staircase.

It was the two huge paintings that hung in the vast dining area to the right that Hannah noticed first. One was of a woman, hanging above a satin green couch, and the other of a gigantic burning sun.

The leopard skin rug with its snarling head, lying on the leather ottoman in front of the green couch, was incredibly striking. Her mother had told her that very much like their own home in Ashby-by-the-Sea, where she herself had grown up with Mini, that she could expect Mini's American home to be filled to the brim with eclectic objects and to expect oddities in the house. Belinda had tried on many occasions to describe the atmosphere and all at once Hannah seemed to grasp it. Enchantment and warmth both emanated throughout the house.

A chandelier with at least a hundred rock crystals hung from the cathedral ceiling, neatly filling the gap by the dramatic staircase.

The crystals' reflections twinkled on a couple of period portraits which hung in the recess of the stairway. The first was of a handsome man dapperly dressed in a suit. The other a woman posing on a chaise lounge, dressed in pearls, wearing a black velvet dress. It was then that Hannah saw the panther on the shelf.

Directly beneath the top of the staircase, on a large deep broad shelf, standing proud was a life-sized copper panther. A painting of the moon hung behind it. Poised and frozen in time the panther's jaw was open, baring its teeth, yet its eyes were soft. The light from the chandelier reflected the copper brilliantly and, in that moment, Hannah felt the hairs on the back of her neck stand up and a chill ran down her spine.

A red waxed sealed envelope on a long-legged table bent Hannah's attention away from the panther. Bleary eyed and seeing it was addressed to her she cracked the wax open. The note inside was instantly recognisable from the letters Hannah had received from Mini over the years. It was written on her personalised stationary, with two engraved palm trees intertwined at the top. It simply read,

Hannah, gone to walk Parky. Make yourself at home darling.

Your bedroom is waiting! Can't wait to see you. Love, Mini x

Surprised and unaware that Mini even had a dog and also slightly perplexed at her lack of attention to greet her summer houseguest, she shrugged off her dismay. In the absence of the hostess, Hannah drifted up the stairs passing the panther on the shelf. Pausing she looked at it again in complete awe. It was magnificent she thought.

At the top of the stairs to the right, on the bedroom door hung a big piece of thick white card suspended by string. The breeze of Hannah's arrival at the door made it flutter on the brass handle. In thick black pen it read,

Welcome Hannah. This is your room for the summer.

A four-poster wooden bed sat in the middle of the bedroom piled high with pillows and the smell of fresh linen filled the air. It looked extremely inviting. Furtling deep into her bag she pulled out a pair of wrinkled up pyjamas, tooth and hairbrush and stepping out of her travel clothes, which she left strewn on the floor, she smirked. Hannah was the 'untidy twin' and even though she no longer shared a bedroom with Amelia back home, she took joy for now in her clothes scattered across the floor. She hopped into her pyjamas and standing in front of a wall mirror stood brushing her long straight blonde hair which now hung limp framing her tiny face. Her tired blue eyes glanced at the reflection behind of an inviting bed and without further ado she ran flopping backwards onto the bed, sinking into the sheets. Within seconds she'd drifted off into a deep sleep.

The next morning, as the light sneaked through the white shutters, more of the bedroom was revealed. Two easy chairs, 'his and hers', in black and white stripes framed the fireplace. Above it hung the portrait of a stylish, blonde haired lady dressed in a bright green sweater, with beautiful red fingernails. Hannah thought it looked like her mother who was also a 'well put together' smart lady. Her father often referred to her as a 'home-maker' and it was true. Her mother was highly organised and committed to the home, Timothy and the girls.

At times, her mother's focus was somewhat oppressive as she ran a tight ship with their 'adopted' Artificial Intelligence family member, designed of course by Timothy, the scientist. It enabled the whole family to flourish. Not only did it give Belinda time to enjoy a mutual interest of art which she shared with Hannah, it also she hoped, instilled a sense of responsibility in the girls and gave them an appreciation for technology whilst, at the same time fostering a mutual respect for all things different.

Taking it all in, Hannah stretched and sprang out of bed.

Eager to see Mini, she skipped and jumped around the room with the excitement one feels on the first day of a holiday. Then pausing, she wondered if she would be able to see the pool and palm trees from her bedroom window that Mini had mentioned in her letters and prized open the shutters of the colonial style house.

The hot morning air had made them stick and they creaked as they opened. As the sun poured through them it made her squint. She could feel its warmth through the glass. The tree's thick green palms wafted in the breeze, regal in their stance. Hannah was astounded that they were the same height as the house. The pool was just as she had imagined. It sparkled and rippled like jelly.

So, on that very first day Hannah ran out of her palatial bedroom, jumping sometimes two steps at a time to the top of the sweeping staircase. Waiting at the bottom with arms outstretched wide and a smile to match was Mini.

After a quick glance at the panther on the shelf, she ran down the stairs falling into her arms and could not help noticing her old-fashioned sweet fragrance. Hannah had only met Mini a couple of times before.

"Good morning. So happy you are finally here," exclaimed Mini, hugging her.

"Breakfast? Tea?"

"Oh, yes please," Hannah replied, looking up at Mini with her arms still wrapped around her waist.

"Oh, morning Parky," Mini said, looking up over her shoulder.

"Parky?" Hannah asked inquisitively.

"The panther on the shelf," she replied.

"The panther?" Hannah replied quizzically, not taking Mini's comment at all seriously.

Mini just winked at her, grabbed her by the hand and led her into an emerald-green tiled kitchen.

Perching on a stool at the end of the kitchen high table Hannah felt the breeze of Mini's Chinese silk dressing gown pass by as breakfast was prepared at speed. Her energy was compelling, she seemed full of light. Hannah had gained a sense of it from the letters she'd received from her, along with the tales she had been told from her mother which Amelia had criticised sarcastically. Less forgiving than Hannah and certainly more judgemental, Amelia's focus like her mother caused her to become irritable and critical at times. Hannah, on the other hand, erred towards her father's disposition. A thinker, with a more relaxed approach to life in general.

"So, first things first. Did you sleep well?" Mini said, scrambling eggs with her back to her. The sweet oily smell of cooking filled the air.

"Such a fabulous friend," she said, out of the blue, rattling on.

Confused, Hannah said, "Pardon?"

"Did you see the portrait above the fireplace in your bedroom? The lady in the green sweater? That's my friend Belinda. I can tell her anything."

Hannah nodded in an agreeable fashion whilst at the same time thinking how Belinda in the portrait really did look like her mother, as she continued to eat her eggs, bewildered by Mini's enthusiasm.

"Well, anyway. We have lots of time to chat about that." Mini said whilst hurriedly cleaning the frying pan.

"I have a lovely day planned for us, Hannah."

Feeling like she was being drawn into the unknown Hannah thought that she was in some way, yet to be clear, beholden to Mini for the summer and in a way, she was rather excited.

Part of that immediate plan was a ride in Mini's car, a 'Thunderbird' nonetheless. Hannah had expected her Grandmother to have a car like that. So, having got ready for the day in her usual tomboy attire of jeans and a t- shirt, Hannah brushed her long blonde hair and waited on the ottoman in the dining room. She sat awkwardly making sure not to sit directly on the leopard skin and stared up at the painting of the woman she had first noticed when she arrived.

It was, she thought, the most beautiful piece of artwork she had ever seen. As a lover of art, mature in attitude and old for her age in many ways, her mother would often say Hannah was a modern day hippy with the looks to match; naturally pretty with tiny proportioned features and speckled with freckles. Unlike Amelia, Hannah was not bothered about beauty or fashion and her slightly scruffy approach added to her tomboy image.

Anyway, the painting she was admiring almost covered the entire wall. In a white flowing skirt, the young woman stood poised in a warrior stance. A gold sword raised in her right hand, as cherubs floated above her head crowning her in a field of flowers, amidst a forest and a stream. A lion was wrapped around her legs, protectively looking lovingly towards her victorious stance. It was quite patriotic in Hannah's opinion.

"Boo!"

Hannah jumped out of her skin at Mini's warm sharp breath on the back of her neck.

"Oh, I'm sorry darling. Quite a dish, don't you think?" Mini said, standing behind her with arms folded,looking smug.

Hannah looked back at the painting, then at Mini and back again.

"Wow, I wouldn't have guessed. I can see now though. Gosh. It's you!"

"A younger me and that's Duchess," Mini said, pointing to the lion.

Hannah looked at her Grandmother, weighing her up. She was a tallish woman for her age, slim framed with chocolate brown hair, which she thought must be dyed, and a smiley round face. She had even dressed the part for a convertible car ride, wearing loose jeans, a red polka dot headscarf and red lipstick.

Looking at Mini, Hannah reflected on the correspondence they had shared over the years. Hannah couldn't help but admire her Grandmother. She was not at all 'granny-like' and had an air of youthful mystery, joie de vivre. She had often thought how much she must have suffered after losing her parents tragically at the age of sixteen and again after being widowed at a young age whilst pregnant with her mother. Despite this tragedy she had nurtured and raised her daughter well in Ashby-by-the-Sea. What had puzzled Hannah though was why Mini had bravely decided to relocate to America, just before Amelia and her were born, leaving their mother in a similar position to Mini, at a time when a daughter would have benefited from having her mother close by.

Hannah now realised that it was the close relationship and strong bond that Mini and Belinda had formed, and she would soon learn, their unparalleled trust in The Great Star of the Cosmos that made this transition easier.

So, Grandmother and Granddaughter drove up the 'Palms to Pines' highway towards the naked mountains and watched as the dry dusty desert landscape gradually grew greener the higher they climbed. The sound of the car engine roared. It was a 1966 baby blue convertible with white leather interior and a spindly wooden steering wheel. They chatted very little and when they did, spoke in raised voices above the noise.

The roads were long and narrow, curving on top of each other, cutting into the mountain resembling a layered cake. The views were breath-taking and after about an hour of driving, which Hannah thought went very quickly, they turned into a viewing place with a quaint wooden picnic bench. They sat there with a flask of tea and Mini produced a cake.

The air was cool and it was extremely quiet except for the odd car and motorbike. After idly chatting for a while Mini looked directly into Hannah's eyes, holding both her hands quite tightly whilst leaning forward, quietly said,

"I have a special power, unlike any other. A Mindful Gift and I think you might possess it too, which is the reason why your mother sent you to stay with me." A million thoughts suddenly raced through Hannah's mind. Mini then said something that would change her life forever.

"My imagination can come to life. This is a Gift that has been granted to me by The Great Star of the Cosmos. I am known as a Gifted One."

Mindfully Gifted, Mini's imagination could stir incredible energy, enabling whatever she imagined coming to life. The only condition being, 'only if she truly believed it could.'

Hannah sat dumbfounded yet in an odd way she was not all surprised.

"Watch me," Mini said.

Suddenly, a huge tunnel of light appeared to beam out from the middle of her chest. Hannah sat with her eyes wide open and mouth gaping. She was astonished but not at all frightened.

"Hannah, close your eyes and join me. I'm conjuring up a truly magnificent sight. I can see Parky the panther flying towards me in the distance!"

Try as she might and squinting, whilst peeking at the spellbinding light pouring from Mini, Hannah just couldn't visualise the spectacle of the life-sized copper panther that stood proudly on the shelf.

This was because even though she was Mindfully Gifted she didn't yet know it. She would need to discover faith in her Gift, *'because to see you have to truly believe'*.

It didn't seem long before all the brightness had faded and Mini had returned back to her normal, but somewhat euphoric, state.

Later, in the car on the way home she would describe how she had imagined Parky flying towards her in a blaze of glory, with huge white angelic wings and the whooshing sound and wind created as he drew close. How he'd landed with quite a thud on the picnic table to then show her such abundant love by rubbing his head against hers in a cattish way.

"Do you know why birds sing Hannah?" Mini said later, trying to explain her Gift.

"Birds sing because they see such wonderful things whilst flying, that when they land all they can do is sing."

That helped explain Mini's aura of happiness and would hopefully help Hannah to figure out if she possessed such a power as The Mindful Gift.

It seemed like a long journey home for Hannah as she was

trying to understand and make sense of the remarkable other world her Grandmother had shared with her. Feeling a mixture of nerves and excitement, Mini then lightened the chatter of Hannah's mind,

"I bet you think it's all '*highfalutin gobbledygook*', don't you?" she asked.

Hannah did not know what to think and arriving back home she scrambled up the wooden staircase, pausing at Parky. Did she also possess The Gift?

Butterflies fluttered in her tummy. She ran into her bedroom flopping onto the bed landing on the gigantic pile of pillows. She began to stare deep in thought at the portrait above the fireplace of Belinda, the lady in the green sweater with the beautiful red nails, whom Mini had said was a great confidante. It still reminded her of her own mother.

Before long a cloudy haze began to cover the portrait and Belinda larger than life emerged from the painting, floating towards Hannah.

Hovering above, whilst resting her head on her knuckles she whispered in a smoky voice, "You have many strange days ahead of you, Hannah. You'll encounter new experiences and new friends but listen to your Grandmother. I will always be here for you if you need to talk. There is still so much you don't know..."

She even sounded eerily like her Mother.

"Can we talk now?" Hannah asked, eagerly sitting upright and unafraid. Belinda though drifted away almost being vacuumed in a haze back into the portrait.

Throughout the apparition Hannah felt her body was in a perpetual glow exuding light, just as Mini's had only hours before. Perhaps she possessed the power to be Mindfully Gifted? She lay in a warmth she had never experienced before, and that same warmth carried her off into a deep sleep.

So, that summer Hannah and Mini's relationship flourished, as the bond between them grew. Now knowing and understanding more about her Grandmother as a person, she was excited at the prospect of sharing and experiencing new adventures with her over the summer.

Being a twin herself Hannah wondered if she might meet Mini's twin. Seldom mentioned by the family, all she really knew about her aunt was that when Mini moved away to England to marry, she had stayed in America. Hannah felt intrigued and could somehow relate to their relationship with one another, when on occasion she had been mentioned by her Mother.

Afternoons rolled into evenings and the two would always conclude the day sitting poolside on a rocking chair that Hannah had playfully named, swing-boat. It was here that Mini would carefully share with Hannah her past and the stories that her imagination had created. It was gradually dawning upon Hannah that the characters in her stories were the exact same objects in the house and unbeknown to her as she sat listening, this newfound and powerful gifted imagination that had been given freely to her was enabling them all to become crystallised within her own mind. Magical beyond belief, whilst listening Hannah would stare up at the night sky.

There seemed to be a piece of sky that held more stars than any other shining down upon her Grandmother's house.

What Hannah didn't know or understand was, '*for where there is good there is always evil*'.

Mini hadn't even told her yet about the powerful dark force of The Mindful Watchers.

'It was then that Hannah saw the panther on the shelf.'

CHAPTER TWO

THE WATCHERS

THE MINDFUL Watchers, who were once Gifted Ones were equally powerful. Sadly though, they had allowed their Gift to become shrouded in darkness. It was very much a case of Good versus evil. Many had joined The Watch because they had lost faith and belief in their Gift meaning they were no longer able to enjoy the true happiness that The Great Star of the Cosmos had intended for them. Like a virus of the mind, The Watchers had let the darkness slowly contort and control them in every possible way. Draining every ounce of colour from their lives.

Ruthlessly, they were determined to use their dark force to put an end to The Gifted Ones extraordinarily Mindful joy.

Letting the darkness control their imaginations, they took pleasure in observing and spying on The Gifted Ones. They held a power to detect their Mindful energy and cruelly destroy aspects of their imaginations forever.

Over the years they had developed a particular style of emanating darkness. Their homes imitated horror movie architecture, black slate roofs, pointed turrets and the occasional seated gargoyle. Their choice of uniform was not much different. Dress code: Black.

It was a huge undertaking for The Gifted Ones being constantly on guard, looking out for The Watchers. Protecting their Gift was relentless.

Watchers were selective about who to prey upon. Drawn to Gifted Ones they were most familiar with capitalised their power.

Mini described the male Watcher that stalked her. His name was Victor Traverse and he lived in the nearby Watchers neighbourhood. Dressed in heavy jeans with a thick sturdy belt and boots, his open necked shirt revealed a crow pendent hanging on his leather necklace. His face was as pointed as the beak of the crow upon his chest. His head was bald, as shiny as a cue- ball, with small eyes set into his face, as deep and dark as parts of the ocean no-one would ever want to go to.

It saddened Mini that Victor had defected to The Watchers and enabled his Gift to grow dark. She felt it was around the time she had discovered her Gift that a higher darker power had engulfed him. The had shared many happy memories being the same age and growing up together. His parents Wallis and Bertie were 'Naturals.' A term that both The Watchers and The Gifted Ones unknowingly both used. Everyone was born with the potential to receive The Gift; however, Naturals were quite simply people free of imaginary power.

Wallis and Bertie were Mini and her sister's Godparents. Portraits of them both which Hannah had admired upon her arrival, graced the walls in the stair well.

Mini loved them like her own parents, who had sadly died suddenly. Following their deaths Wallis and Bertie embraced both girls into their lives and as Naturals were able to protect the girls, who hadn't yet fully discovered their Gift, albeit briefly from The Watchers.

The Watchers dark Gifted power wrapped over themselves, a false blanket of security. Becoming accustomed to their self-focused, blinkered view of the world, their still powerful imaginations had lost the non-judgemental open mindedness intended for them. Narrow minded in approach they were known in Gifted circles as Watchercrows. An evolution of evil enabled them with the ability to transform into one of the most intelligent and probably adaptable of all the bird species, the crow. Enabling them to prey upon their victims.

So, on a dark rainy day, which was unusual for the city of Palms, Mini lit a fire and snuggling under a couple of cosy blankets began to tell Hannah more about The Mindful Watchers as well as Parky, the panther and other friends.

A Gifted Ones imaginary friends became crystallised in their minds through the memories and experiences encountered of life's important, as well as joyful events. It was by being receptive and trusting in The Great Star of the Cosmos, that brought these friends, with their own specific powers to life.

Mini explained that when she was a girl, about Hannah's age, probably a year older, following her parents death and with their godparents blessing, that she had met the real life Parky as a helping hand in the travelling circus that ran the route of the Midwest train line. They had bonded instantly and both be- friended a leopard called Pentheus. The three were inseparable during those days. They played and even slept together on the straw circus beds. She was the only handler in the circus crew who could do this, leaving many members revering her. Both leopard and panther followed her everywhere. She led them out to walk like poodles on long glamorous leashes. It was Mini's intense friendship with the big cats that crystallized them both in her mind. The copper panther on the shelf and the leopard skin on the ottoman were purchased later on in her life, to keep them alive in her imagination.

The sun and moon painting were actually purchased by Mini's father, William Cernobbio. His love of art had clearly passed through the generations and it was this love of not only art but of light that led him to commission two pieces of work from a local bohemian artist. With this adoration of light he stipulated that one should be of a burning sun and the other of a moon. Mini often wondered if her parents were Gifted but regrettably she had never found out.

Mini went on to tell Hannah that on one occasion when she had brought Parky and the burning sun painting to life, she had also awakened The Watchers cavernous depths of darkness. Their suspicious nature caused many Watchercrows to encircle her house like vultures. The burning sun painting had cast such an incredible light upon Parky that his copper body shone intensely.

In that moment Parky came alive. He began to shake his head, flap his ears and point his chin upwards. He growled peering around. His sorrowful eyes saw the Watchercrows beaks tapping vigorously upon the window. As they did, he lifted his paw, the shelf creaked as it always did when he first moved and his eyes narrowed into a mean stare towards them. He thrust his chest forward and began sprouting the most beautiful thick white lustrous wings, transforming into a winged panther.

Leaping off the shelf, his wings extended and breaking through the large square window that framed the chandelier before it, he climbed high into the sky, mighty in flight, fighting off the Watchercrows' beaks that pecked him constantly. White wings, black Watchercrows speckled the skyline. As many as one hundred of them hung from his gigantic wings beating him down in his quest. Exacerbated and knowing they were close to victory in destroying him from Mini's imagination forever, Parky's eyes began to well with tears.

It was the intense light from The Great Star of the Cosmos that saved him that day, warding off the Watchercrows, as they dispersed like dust. The same light that would one day save his life.

Before returning to his shelf Parky wrapped his gigantic wings around Mini as they were once again united, safe in her beautiful mind having been moments away from being destroyed completely by The Watchers.

When Mini had finished reciting her story a tear rolled down Hannah's cheek. These imaginary friends were intrinsically part of Mini's Gifted world.

Hannah listened intently when Mini told her about the floor lamp in the dining area. Having the body of Greek goddess holding a liberty torch, Mini explained that she was her beacon of light, always keeping a watch out. She had been named it after her own mother, Nancy. Coincidently it had originally been purchased from an antique store from a place called Nancy in France.

Mini recalled how her mother had told her to always let her light shine for others to see. Another reason Mini would often think why her parents have been Gifted.

It was the owl at the top of the stairs that Mini didn't dwell on. Hannah had noticed it when making her way to her bedroom. A wooden friendly faced chap. Mini nodded and had simply muttered, 'an interesting fella.'

A bystander being enveloped in a whole new world, Hannah decided from that moment onwards that she would try to see things from a different perspective and find her Gift. If indeed she possessed it.

It was later in the day and Hannah was pacing the black and white diamond floor tiles in the hallway, Mindfully thinking about all she had been told. Suddenly the tiles underneath her feet began to rise up and down, undulating like an old-fashioned town fair ride. The Cakewalk.

Feeling strangely warm, Hannah's imagination had started to

come to life because she was starting to believe in her Gift. She knew that what was happening to her was exactly what she had witnessed happening to Mini up in the mountains and to herself earlier when she had seen Belinda from the portrait. Hannah felt her heart swell as light poured out of her chest and she wondered to herself how this power might look like to others.

Pentheus the leopard who resided on the ottoman was stirring. He cracked his jaw and neck, raising his back into a high cat stretch whilst extending each leg, one at a time, reminiscent of a ballerina warming up. He peered over at Hannah with inquisitive kind eyes and then glanced up at Mini's painting that had come to life.

Duchess the lion was rubbing herself in a feline manner around young Mini's legs as she turned towards Hannah winking and smiling proudly. Golden sword raised high in her hand in an Amazonian stance she was content the hour of Hannah's revelation had arrived. The water in the background of the painting flowed freely.

The sun painting began sprouting flames and in the corner of the room a tall liberty floor lamp, in the form of a beautiful goddess holding a torch, suddenly spoke,

"Pleased to meet you," curtsying, holding the torch upright, "I'm Nancy." Looking quite distressed, she said with a drawling accent, "Oh dear, it's chaos when we all ignite and I just don't know what's going to happen with Miss Mini if those crows come knocking again."

The house was coming alive and Hannah felt her energy rising. The moon painting above Parky had oil dripping from the crevasses of the moon. Parky on his shelf started swishing his tail and the portraits on the stairs were now stepping out of their frames. The portrait of the lady followed by the young man who extended his hand leading her down the stairs.

"Hello," nodding her head to Hannah, "I'm Wallis." "Greetings," the young man chipped in, "Bertie."

The owl that stood right at the top of the staircase was flapping insanely and by now Parky had jumped off the shelf and was prowling around in a protective manner. He kept looking up at Hannah with slit eyes and ears back. Then his expression would rapidly change from curious to fearful. Hannah couldn't keep her eyes off him and felt an immediate bond with him as though she was destined to befriend him.

"Stations I say!" Pentheus the leopard barked loudly, the tone reverberated around the hall. He seemed to be taking charge of the action unfolding. Then bumping into Hannah said, "Oh, excuse me," then coughed, "Pleased to meet you my dear," extending a fur paw. He was incredibly well spoken and had an old-fashioned manner.

Closing in behind Hannah, Parky nudged her legs and she toppled onto his back.

"Sit still," he said, turning his head around as he launched himself with a mighty jump back onto the shelf.

She could see it all from here, a house full of imaginative chaos. It was all so exciting. Nancy the lamp was wobbling, trying to peer through the blinds for potential Watchers, making the torch she carried flicker.

Dismounting Parky Hannah sat by his side and her legs dangled over the shelf.

"These are your friends now Hannah," Parky said, sitting upright beside her also spectating the goings on. His voice was deep and meaningful. Then, looking directly at her he said,

"*Only if you believe with your full heart can your imagination come to life,*" reminding her to visit her new friends often.

Hannah leant her head on his shoulder, then closing her eyes said, "Of course I will."

When she opened her eyes, she was sitting on the bottom step of the stairs and perching by her was Mini.

"Welcome to my world Hannah. Tell me everything."

'His head was bald, as shiny as a cue-ball, with small eyes set into his face, as deep
and dark as parts of the ocean no-one would ever want to go.'

CHAPTER THREE

SPYGLASS HILL DRIVE

MINI, INTRIGUED by what Hannah was telling her listened intently. Eyebrows slightly raised, brown eyes wide open and mouth agape she was fascinated by what was being euphorically recited about her first epic imaginative journey. It was Parky who Mini was most enthralled by.

"He's a precious part of my imagination as well, Hannah." Mini knew his extraordinary power and was so pleased that Hannah had also been chosen by The Great Star to experience this for herself.

Hannah was impatient with her new Gift and naturally wanted to relive her experience again and again. However, it was now night-time and she was exhausted by the events of her incredible day. Hugging Mini she decided to head up to bed. It wasn't long before she was asleep, falling into a deep dream.

In the dream, a bright light filled the bedroom creating a vast sky. Part of the light separated into colours forming an arch, a rainbow. At the top of the arch was Parky beckoning Hannah towards him with his paw. Beyond him and the rainbow there were dark thunderous clouds, many of them heavy in precipitation, moving and constantly forming. "Come Hannah, come," he said, a voice as deep as before, with velvet undertones echoing in the dark sky.

The darker the sky became the brighter the rainbow colours shone. Hannah started to climb the rainbow staircase and along the way many of the new imaginary friends floated by lifelessly. Nancy the lamp passed by bobbing up and down, as though she was in choppy water. Pentheus the leopard was all legs as he tumbled through the air cartwheeling. For a moment Hannah felt she wanted to turnaround and head back down the rainbow.

At the top of the arch, Parky stood waiting with eyes full of love but his face was full of anguish. The dark clouds behind him were closing in and his expression turned to that of sadness and loss of control. The rainbow beneath them began to fade. Hannah could feel herself falling. Reaching her hands out towards Parky she felt the weight of the world dragging her down. Below her, fire and flames were sprouting up from the ground.

Terrified, Hannah screamed. Then from out of the flames appeared an upright sword followed by a body. It was the younger Mini from the painting. The flames began to disperse and Hannah landed effortlessly on the ground. Glowing before her stood Mini. Skirt rippling in the breeze and Duchess the lion by her side.

"Ready for battle?" she asked. Her face now seemed to have changed to that of her Grandmother.

It was evident that both the paintings of Belinda and the younger Mini were beginning to crystallise themselves as new imaginary friends.

The dream was over.

Hannah, wide awake sat bolt upright. Her long hair was moist and tangled from beads of sweat. Lying back on the pillows the chatter from her mind left her feeling saddened, disturbed yet intrigued. What was the darkness beyond the rainbow? The Mindful Watchers? Was that Mini her Grandmother in the dream, or was it the younger Mini from the painting?

Staring at the portrait of Belinda, Hannah's energy was beginning to rise, igniting her imagination. Aware of a huge tunnel of light radiating from deep within her Belinda was being brought to life.

Before long, a cloudy haze began to cover the portrait, "You've come a long way," Belinda said, hovering and resting her head on her knuckles.

Hannah's words came tumbling out, "I've been dreaming frightful dreams. I think Parky could be trouble with The Mindful Watchers."

"The Mindful Watchers are extremely dangerous, Hannah," warned Belinda, "are you sure you want to venture into the darkness when you're enjoying the light so much?"

"If I don't, I could risk losing the light and losing my new imaginary friends."

Belinda had now swelled in size, "Talk with your Grandmother," her husky tones echoed, resembling her size. Lastly "Hannah, remember this," her voice now fading as she was being sucked hazily back into the portrait,

"Only if you believe with your full heart, can your imagination come to life."

With those words she was frozen back in time.

Feeling her own brightness fade, Hannah paused, now fully appreciating the intense power of her Mindful Gift. She realised how important it was to continue to have faith and truly believe in it, particularly now as the quest to find out about The Watchers had begun. It would prove to be harder than she ever could have thought.

For a moment it felt surreal, being enveloped in this new imaginary world. It was so detached from the reality of her life in Ashby-by-the-Sea.

Feeling a real sense of homesickness, and accompanying vulnerability she had the sense of being dragged down. Why me? Why not Amelia, was she Gifted too? She thought.

Gradually the sudden intensity and merry-go-round of emotions settled. First things first she would follow Belinda's advice.

In the shimmering emerald kitchen the following morning, Mini and Hannah discussed in great depth a plan of how to investigate The Watchers. Hannah also spoke about their meeting in the dream and seeing her Grandmothers face appear as the young mini in the painting.

"I have an idea," Mini winked. Hannah remained surprised at her Grandmother's abundant energy.

"We can now speak with each other through our imaginations, even if we aren't near one another."

"Could be useful in our fight against The Watchers," Hannah said.

"The burning sun painting can be an indication from you to me that you need help, but we must remember The Watchers can detect our Mindful energy. They would head directly to the source, destroying whatever we are imagining, so we have to be skilful."

Pondering Mini's words, Hannah's instinct was telling her that she needed to practice her skills more.

Halting at the bottom of the staircase and turning to the shelf she stared at Parky, "Time to play," she thought, but there was to be no playing for Hannah. She was learning that her powerful Gift was not an on-off button. She was expecting a miracle to think that her imagination would ignite without her whole heart believing, as Parky had reminded her.

Try as she might Hannah could not make her imagination come to life. She was no more than a resounding gong because she wasn't believing with her whole heart. She was playing, making a mockery of her Gift. It was a sore lesson to learn. Her faith was fading and she struggled with self-doubt. It was hard as well for Mini watching, as she would peek in on Hannah and knew exactly what she was trying to do. Lessons had to be learnt.

Standing in the hallway in front of the high, white, double vaulted doors, holding her mackintosh, Hannah glanced up at Parky on the shelf and took a deep long sigh. Would she ever be able to hone her power and recreate him?

Fed up, frustrated and totally despondent she decided to take herself for a long walk. Head hung low she ventured out of the doors and in doing so felt she was letting the drawbridge down on a magical castle.

After walking for a while the air became cooler. Hannah was glad that she had grabbed her mackintosh thinking that this was either because of the time of day or maybe because she had left the warmth of Mini's home.

As she walked she wondered why this was so. Mini's home held a warmth that was indescribable, perhaps the same kind of glow you feel when you are happy. She would later come to realise that it was the aura of being a Gifted One. Anyway, before long after walking quite far she knew she had arrived in Watcherland, The Watchers neighbourhood.

The homes were just as Mini had described. Black slate roofs and pointed turrets, some had long narrow gardens in front of them with iron gates at the top. Other houses were closer to the road.

Shivered by the cool air and the austere surroundings she wrapped her blue coloured mackintosh tightly around her. Pulling up the hood she turned her head, spotting a sign on a tall thin pole. 'Spyglass Hill Drive.'

A few houses up the Drive a man was pottering in his garden. He was dressed and looked just as Mini had described in heavy black jeans, thick sturdy belt, open necked shirt and boots. Was that Victor? He gave a cursory glance towards Hannah, squinting his eyes, then returned to what he was doing.

Surprisingly the occasional house had colour. A yellow frayed curtain here, a deep-red letterbox there, set against the exterior building work of smokey-grey with black brick it was quite a contrast. More noticeably in one of the long thin gardens and close to the house was a citrus fruit grove.

Looking over each shoulder to check if anyone was looking, Hannah decided to walk into the fruit grove. It was most odd she thought that fruit could grow in such a cool climate.

Glancing up at the house and intermittently checking around she tiptoed down the path, hunching her shoulders over as she went. Her tomboyish nature had gotten the better of her and feeling naughty she nervously chuckled to herself at the prospect of taking an orange or two.

The ripe fruit was a blaze of citrus colours and a mysterious warmth in the air wrapped around the grove. Picking an orange Hannah was momentarily transfixed and she heard a tapping at the window of the house. The noise came from one of the small square windows at the top.

The face of an old woman appeared behind half drawn, torn, silver-grey curtains, she held a somewhat familiar, yet curious expression.

Spooked, by the engagement and dropping the orange, Hannah ran scared away from the grove and up the cracked pavers towards the top of the hill. Feeling breathless she slowed down trying to get her breath back. whilst resting her hands on her waist.

"You ok?" she heard a young man's voice ask.

Crouching in the porch of one of the houses to the left of the drive was a young man fixing his motorbike. Unable to reply, due to her breathlessness, Hannah nodded a yes.

"Come and take a seat," he said, kindly pointing to the step of the porch. "I'm Tom."

"Thanks, I'm Hannah," as she gladly, yet cautiously, due to being in Watcherland, took a seat.

He was handsome, tall, athletically built, with jet black wavy hair, and was dressed in black jeans and a black leather jacket. Probably a couple of years older than herself, she thought. Hannah flushed, the sensation of a flurry of butterflies danced inside her tummy as she shyly gazed into his eyes. They were a deep chocolate colour and his skin was extremely pale making his dark eyes protrude.

He resumed work on his motorbike, frequently peering at Hannah out of the corner of his eye, whilst smiling tightly. Hannah couldn't help noticing that hanging on the motorbike was a unicorn keyring.

Sensing she was staring, Tom shyly moved in front of it and for a moment the situation became awkward, his initial charming attributes seemed to be covering a nervousness.

Hannah needed to find out more, not only about Tom but also about the old woman in the window. She was in the heart of Watcherland.

'*She turned her head, spotting a sign on a tall thin pole Spyglass Hill Drive.*'

CHAPTER FOUR

MAKING THE IMPOSSIBLE POSSIBLE

WITHOUT A doubt Hannah thought Tom was charming and her concerns about him being a potential Watcher soon got absorbed into making pleasantries. Tom asked Hannah where she lived, despite already knowing the answer and already having knowledge of her Grandmother.

Both were deeply aware of their differences, yet this only added to the excitement of this initial encounter. Both of them knew they were Mindfully Gifted. Eventually Hannah being quite direct steered the chat towards the unicorn keyring. It was hanging from his motorbike and she felt a sense of mystery about it. Tom clearly didn't want to talk about it avoiding the subject altogether.

"I'll finish fixing my motorbike and maybe I could take you for a ride?" he suddenly volunteered.

Hannah, without hesitation nodded keenly.

"Do you have a name for your motorbike?" she asked. "Hawk," replied Tom.

Hannah's mind began to wander and as she waited, she began thinking how long it had been since she'd left home. With no watch and no phone, she sat trying to work out how long the walk had taken her from Mini's and then the time she had spent since. She'd been gone for a couple of hours she guessed and Mini would be wondering where she was, except she knew exactly where Hannah had gone; in search of The Mindful Watchers.

Patiently waiting at home, Mini was intermittently checking in with her Gift, watching the burning sun painting. If she saw a glimpse of a fireball Hannah would be imagining it as well and that was the sign she was in trouble.

"Tom, could you give me a ride back home please? I can direct you, it's not that far from here," she knew then at least she'd be on her way.

"Urgh, I tend to ride up in the mountains," he replied.

"What, those mountains?" she said pointing to the beautiful Bretalina range; the ones that Mini had previously driven her to.

"Yes, are you coming?" he asked.

Hit with a dilemma, Hannah wasn't one to look a gift horse in the mouth. She felt torn; as much as she wanted to venture up into the mountains again, she knew the right thing to do was to go back home to Mini.

"Can I come back tomorrow? my Grandmother will be worried

as I've been out for a while now." Hannah felt protective over Mini, even though she was used to living alone being fiercely independent.

So, they agreed, same place but at an earlier time the next day. Hannah had made the decision to walk home.

"Really nice to meet you," Tom said warmly, and they awkwardly shook hands in a clumsy fashion.

Behind Tom, over their handshake Hannah noticed that the unicorn keyring was gleaming, swaying forwards and backwards on its chain. For a moment the cool Watcher air seemed to disperse around them, and a warmth radiated between the pair.

She looked up at Tom, flushed and replied, "You too!"

With a skip and a jump as she always did when she became excited, Hannah skipped happily down SpyGlass Hill Drive, finally on her way back to Mini.

It was starting to get dusk and Hannah's mind was brimming with questions about The Mindful Watchers that she wanted to ask Tom. Whilst walking she began to daydream, picturing herself riding with him on the back of his motorbike into the mountains, confiding deeply with each other in one another's Gifts whilst Tom was putting his arm around her.

All of a sudden, she became fully aware that it was twilight and to her left she saw an array of muted colourful tones. It was the citrus grove at the old woman's house.

The fruit had multiplied, having dropped to the floor in abundance. Peering up at the same window as before, she noticed a warm lamp flickering, revealing the shadow of a head standing behind the silver-grey torn curtains. Nervously not wanting to make eye contact again Hannah quickly diverted her glance, quickened her pace and headed home.

As Hannah approached Mini's, the house stood proud and soft lighting lit up each and every window. As she opened the high, white, double vaulted doors the chandelier twinkled and the familiar warmth along with the smell of her Grandmother's old-fashioned fragrance filled the air.

Clumsily, kicking off her shoes and glancing up at Parky she felt so happy to be home that her heart began to swell and light unexpectedly poured out from her chest. Her powerful imagination had started to ignite!

The chandelier began to shine with extreme intensity and as it reflected upon Parky, his copper-coloured coat transformed into a liquid state that began to crystallise into a million sparkles. He was coming alive.

His head hung low, purring undertones vibrated around the room. He moaned and turning his head slowly to her smiled with loving eyes. He raised his left paw off the shelf that creaked as it always did and hissed, "Hannah," in a deep, slow voice that boomed and reverberated around the room.

He leapt off the shelf to where she was standing and nudging her legs with his head, whilst slinking by her, she toppled onto his back. Wrapping her arms around his neck she felt utter happiness, love but most of all relief and gratitude that her Mindful Gift had once again returned; she was home and with Parky.

"Hold tight, *only if you believe, can you make the impossible possible.*"

With those meaningful words he thrust his chest forward and began sprouting the most beautiful, thick, white lustrous wings, transforming into a winged panther just as Mini had described.

Full of awe and sitting tightly upon his streamlined back she adjusted her legs around his wings, which by now were filling the hallway knocking off Mini's ornaments and making pictures crash to the floor. She bent forward and touched his feathers. They were coarse and whiter than snow.

Suddenly, as if by magic the high, white, double vaulted doors flung open. Tucking in his wings tightly, Parky bolted; running out of the doors, picking up speed very quickly as panthers do. Holding on around his neck, the wind rushed through Hannah's hair as she tried to catch her breath hardly able to keep her eyes open as it made her face ripple. Then with a gigantic upwards leap they were flying!

Feeling not at all fearful and extremely safe, this mutual trust paved the way to a blissful state of peace. Confidence was instilled in her, creating a feeling that nothing else in the world mattered.

Soaring together, neither spoke a word. It was the dead of night, the air was still and the night sky was littered with more stars than can be imagined. Then Parky turned his neck. Glancing and smiling at Hannah he said,

"You're a Gifted One, just like Mini, but sadly not all those who are like you want to embrace the beauty and joy their Gift can bring to them."

He was referring of course to The Mindful Watchers.

Hannah looked down. She thought she recognised the view, albeit from a different angle it was instantly identifiable with the black slate roofs and pointed turrets. They were flying much lower now over Watcherland and the air became stale and cool. Parky swooped low, hissed and soared almost vertically.

He knew he couldn't hover for long as Hannah's Mindful energy would stir The Watchers. Even in the dead of night Watchercrows would be out, so they headed home.

Travelling through the night sky it was as though no other soul existed, just Hannah and Parky. The Great Star of the Cosmos had brought their paths together. This unison would endure to create a lasting friendship. One that would change the course of history.

"It's my mission to convert The Watchers, Parky," Hannah boldly announced, leaning forward shouting in his ear. He chirped acknowledging what she'd said, then his huge wings came whooshing down on the balcony of Hannah's bedroom. He landed with a thud, then lowering his head tilted forward and she slid over it.

"Thank you Parky," she said, wrapping her arms around his neck and hugging him extra tightly, as she anxiously remembered her dream in this very same room of him in danger.

"I will help you in your quest," his deep voice uttered, staring directly into her eyes. He then drifted away back into the dark of night to mysteriously return to his shelf.

The next day Hannah was up with the lark pacing the house waiting for the time to go and meet Tom. Joyous following her Mindful experience with Parky she was also feeling apprehensive about discussing The Mindful Watchers with Tom, maybe even a little fearful.

Reassuring her, Mini said, "It'll be more about what you do than what you say," anxiously knowing the journey she was undertaking.

"I'll keep my heart, mind and eyes on that burning sun painting!" Mini said, winking at her. "Just remember Hannah, keep an open mind. Don't carry doubt in your heart but always believe it can and will happen."

Mini knew instinctively that today would be a day of revelation for Hannah. She knew Tom would be able to reveal details about The Watchers that she couldn't. However, for Hannah the drama would begin on her journey to meet him.

'Soaring together, neither spoke a word. It was the dead of night, the air was still and the night sky was littered with more stars than can be imagined.'

CHAPTER FIVE

THE BOOK OF SPELLS

THE WEATHER on Hannah's journey to meet Tom was the most bewildering experience she had ever encountered. Sun, rain, wind and snow.

The beautiful sunny weather leaving Mini's house did not feel unusual. Light and warmth radiated around The Gifted neighbourhoods. The numerous gardens, public spaces and open paths all led to the far plains that lay before the mountains. The sun shone brilliantly, bringing the colours of nature to life, dancing on the heads of the flowers, and where the dew still lay, it created a rainbow effect.

The leaves on the trees were a combination of vibrant green colours; sage, mint, lime and some were a beautiful deep emerald. The grass resembled a green velvet carpet and the palms on the trees were thick and leathery. Everything was in abundance and everything sparkled.

The warmth from the sun felt comforting as it tickled Hannah's skin and the bird song made her walk with a spring in her step. Hummingbirds hovered mid-flight close by. All was good and Hannah took a deep breath closing her eyes in a blissful state. Then out of the blue time seemed to stand still.

Out of nowhere immediately ahead rain was falling hard. Hannah, baffled, stopped still in her tracks. Ahead of her the sky was patchy grey and she could feel a waft of coolness approaching. A galactic haze seemed to frame the image that lay ahead and the smell of rain began to fill the air.

Looking forwards, then backwards and forwards again, she did not know what to do or have a clue what was happening. An unknown force seemed to be drawing her forward and the spray from the rain ahead was now on her face. The heavy droplets of water bounced off the road.

Proceeding unwillingly into the wet zone, within seconds she was drenched. Her trusted jeans began to feel glued to her legs and her pumps squelched as she walked. She began to feel cold and her long blonde hair hung dripping wet. Hannah found herself sobbing uncontrollably, feeling utterly helpless.

As the raindrops made loud clapping noises, crashing to the ground, she wrapped her arms tightly around herself trying to keep warm. Tiptoes became small leaps as the puddles got deeper and her jeans became heavier. Lifting her head to the left and squinting in the rain she noticed she was in Watcherland.

The dark sky made the houses even more imposing. Squeezing her eyes tightly shut she started thinking hard about the burning sun painting and Mini. It was useless. Bottom lip quivering, Hannah wanted to give in and simply curl up in the gutter which was now gushing with water. Staying focused she quickened her pace, keeping her head down, as one does in wet weather, but a strong wind was now pushing against her and getting fiercer with every step.

The rain had subsided, but the wind was getting up. It sounded like a million paper bags rustling. The trees on the sidewalk arched, straining against the pressure. A flurry of leaves began to create several dust devils which swayed independently like spinning tops towards her.

As if by magic the elements were changing as Hannah wandered through the place where The Mindful Watchers lived. Was this a spell? The wind ceased almost instantaneously and feeling bedraggled Hannah stood blinking, open-mouthed, as she stared in disbelief, as all around her was now snow. Deep snow.

The air was still, crisp, fresh and cold. A sparkling white blanket had miraculously landed, creating a 'magical kingdom' effect on the pointed turrets of The Mindful Watchers homes. Not a sound could be heard, except footsteps trudging towards her, crunching in the snow.

A figure wearing a red hooded cape was approaching. Feeling her heartbeat quicken, Hannah rapidly looked around fathoming out her bearings. Relieved, she realised she was not far from Tom's, but then the figure stopped in front of her.

A pair of old hands appeared from under the cape, lowering the hood down gently. It revealed the face of the old woman from the house with the citrus grove. Frightened, Hannah drew in a swift short breath and the woman smiled warmly, reassuringly back at her.

"Hello Hannah," she said gently.

"Hello," Hannah replied cautiously, nervously stuttering about taking the fruit.

"I'm so sorry for picking your fruit, I was hungry you see, and I happened to see your beautiful grove, erm it is your grove, isn't it?" She was so lost in her apology that she didn't notice that the face of the old woman was turning very much into a face she recognised, similar to that of her Grandmother.

"Shhhh," the old woman mouthed, placing her index finger in front of her lips.

There was a familiarity to the face, but then it changed again to that of the old woman, leaving her feeling confused and disorientated.

"Hannah, I am Mindfully Gifted like you, but I live among the Watchers. I know you are on a quest to save Parky, and restore faith among the Watchers, but please never forget this: Once, they believed in their Gift, just as you do. Faith can involve a battle, and you will battle their faith and your own. I will help you, which is why I am giving you this Gift."

The snow was beginning to melt, and the old woman's gift was a tiny book. Small enough to fit into the palm of a hand, it was red, leather bound with gilt edging and a golden clasp. Placing the tiny book into the palm of Hannah's hand, the old woman placed hers on top of it and looking directly into her eyes said, "It's a Book of Spells Hannah, only to be opened in life or death circumstances. Keep it safe."

Standing at the gate of the old woman's house, Hannah nodded firmly having understood the instructions and watched her as she walked back up the long path to her house. The grove was brimming with fruit and a warm light radiated through the windows as the woman approached her house. Turning around and looking over her shoulder, the old woman waved and went inside.

Hannah put the Book of Spells into her pocket, noticing the snow had completely gone, but the cool air remained.

Despite feeling overwhelmed by the experience and wanting to retreat back to her Grandmother's, Hannah's sheer determination remained. "Time to meet Tom," she thought.

So, after a few minutes walking she could see him ahead, leaning on his motorbike in front of the porch.

"Am I late?" she asked.

"Dead on time," he replied, looking down at his watch.

"Phew, what a morning! Wasn't the weather awful?" Hannah said fiddling with her hair, hoping she was presentable while at the same time brushing off her jeans, which by now were bone dry.

"It's always the same here," Tom replied, cocking his right brow, "Always grey, always cool."

It dawned upon Hannah that only she'd experienced the weather phenomenon.

"Are you ready?" Tom asked, swinging his leg over the motorbike whist putting his hand out towards Hannah to join him.

"Come on Hannah, let's fly!" The unicorn keyring shone brighter than ever.

She held on, arms wrapped tightly around Tom's black leather jacket as they sped off.

The cool air streamed through her hair. Bending into the corners, they turned at considerable speed following the same route Mini had taken up the Bretalina mountain range. They also stopped at the same viewing place, with the same wooden picnic bench. It was like déjà vu.

"I have to run away to the mountains to enjoy my Gift...I'm Mindfully Gifted too, Hannah. But I think you already knew that."

"I thought you might be," Hannah replied, knowing that Tom lived among The Watchers.

"My parents can't detect my mindful energy up here. If they caught me using my Gift, they would destroy it. It's been lonely, using it on my own...but maybe that ends today?" he said, putting his hand on top of Hannah's. Mmmm, charming, she thought.

"Tom, can you tell me about The Watchers please? I need to understand why they lean to the dark side. I want to help. I want to protect."

Tom's eyes narrowed and he sighed deeply,

"I'll tell you everything later. Let's share our gifts together first."

His charming plea filled Hannah with compassion and feeling her energy rising, she knew she was about to share a Mindful experience with Tom.

'Small enough to fit into the palm of a hand, it was leather bound in red with gilt edging and a golden clasp.'

CHAPTER SIX

THE GREAT GIFTED NICKOLOUS

Years of living in the darkness of Watcherland had infused in Tom a fear that was choking the light and life from his very being, creating a nervous self-doubt.

He had good heart, but worried that his lack of faith would one day result in him losing his imagination completely.

Born and bred amongst The Watchers it had been instilled in him from an early age not to trust being a Gifted one. It was easy to see why he found freedom with Hannah. In her was a pure innocence that he had yearned for his entire life.

As an only child, Tom had a fairly solitary existence. Raised in a traditional Watcher household, his parents Richard and Margaret Keys strictly abided by the Watcher Crowcode blinded by the illusion of control. Children of Watchers rarely played outside and spent the majority of their days cooped up inside.

Tom had tried to stay under the radar by not joining the various groups and councils which were the only real form of social interaction Watchers could participate in and seemed to enjoy.

Many an hour was spent deciding who to Watch, when to Watch and where to Watch amongst The Gifted Ones.

'Who's Watching Who,' was their slogan.

Their lives were introspective lacking creativity and any form of individualism was to be frowned upon.

Tom worried about many things, including the profound gloom and sadness he felt dragging him down on a daily basis. Believing he was different to all his Watcher friends, his singular enjoyment in life was his motorbike which fed from a fascination as a young child with small auto toys. An interest partly encouraged by Watcher parents, to keep boys focused on where they were going and what to Watch.

As young boy, he would trade small toy cars, the ones he was allowed at least, with other Watcher boys. It was commonplace to do this but kept secret from the Elders, the name the boys used for grown up Watchers. If his toy car allowance had exceeded the small quota of cars allowed, he would hide the remainder under his bed. This provoked a feeling of guilt that he considered he shouldn't be harbouring.

He longed for an open relationship with his parents and desperately wanted to share his true feelings with them, but he couldn't. He often thought they may feel the same way and he wondered if they 'went along' with the perception of being model Watchers.

Then there were The Watcher girls. Tom wanted a girlfriend who he could be himself with. Someone independent of thought, creative and colourful.

The Watcher-girls were all beautiful, at least on the outside, but lacked depth. They had hidden shallows; birdbaths were deeper.

The only exciting individual attribute they had to offer, as far as he was concerned was the way they personalised their black gypsy style skirts, some short and some long and blouses, with crow adornments made from either jewellery or feathers.

In Tom's eyes the girls lacked individuality, all looking the same.

When The Watcher girls were with you, they weren't really with you and seemed blank and expressionless. Self-interest and focus occupied their spiteful suspicious personalities refined from childhood. A sad and yet interesting terrain of their personas was the ability to gossip in their 'Watcher Voyeur' society.

So, all this led to an insecure and unstable environment to grow up and live in.

It was with a sense of relief and happiness for Tom that day at the viewing point on the Bretalina mountain range when Hannah's energy began to rise; it was clear she was beginning to master her imagination and was a dream come true for Tom and the freedom he found in her brought a tear to his eye.

A huge tunnel of light poured from her chest and looking over at Tom she could see the light pouring from his as well. Taking his hand, she smiled joyfully, their joint gratitude had deepened their faith and Gifts.

"Remember I told you my motorbike's name was Hawk?" Tom said, prompting her imagination, "I would be honoured Miss, if you would fly with me today."

Hannah closed her eyes. Her energy had risen to its peak and when she opened them, before her stood a huge prehistoric looking bird. Its plumage was bright white, and its shoulders, thighs and wing linings were black. It was a hawk and its strong hooked beak was terrifying. Even though its eyes were piercing there was a familiarity about them. It was of course Tom.

"Don't be afraid, climb onto my back," he said, thinking how he had always wished of doing this with a girlfriend.

Hannah, taking a deep breath ran and leapt onto his back.

Turning his giant head, Tom squawked and digging his razor edge talons into the dusty ground pushed off into flight.

It was without doubt exhilarating and Hannah cheered at the top of her voice. It was peaceful too gliding in the mountains and the view of the desert floor was both serene and eerie. She felt safe astride Tom soaring in the sky, but something felt odd, she wondered if her imagination was slipping.

Later she would realise that it was a doubtful fear subconsciously choking her imagination because in the far distance that day she could see a flock of crows circling. "Tom!" Hannah shouted, holding on tightly. "Look, can you see the crows circling?"

Tom, in his peripheral vision could see her pointing in the direction of the crows and his eyes narrowed. It was Watchercrows. They both felt their imaginations instantly fade and, in a flash, they were back on the ground leaning against Tom's motorbike.

Heads down, Hannah could see Tom was bitterly disappointed. "I'm sorry Tom," she said, putting her arm around him.

"I'm sorry, Hannah. The Mindful Watchers were detecting our energy. I have to stop them, but I'm scared to try." His head hung in shame.

Hannah placed her hand on top of Tom's. "You don't have to do it alone. Tell me all about them, and we can do this together."

For the next hour or two the pair sat side by side with their backs leant up against a rock. Luckily, Tom had basic provisions of soda and snacks that he kept in a box on his motorbike and Hannah wasn't in any rush.

"Hannah you can't tell anyone, and I mean anyone," he warned fearfully.

"Tom," She said profoundly. "You can trust me. I have complete faith in my Gift now, even though it's still new. I'm learning. It's brought me such love and joy and I want to protect it. The only way we can fight the Watchers together is if you have complete faith in your Gift, too."

With a tight smile Tom kept nodding, agreeing with her, but Hannah began to sense that she may not be able to trust him.

For some reason she felt the need to reach inside her pocket for the Book of Spells. Feeling it was there she was reassured and settled down against the rock with her arms folded and said, "Anyway, your turn Tom, tell me about The Watchers."

"Myth has it that The Great Gifted Nickolous created the darkness and The Mindful Watchers of today.

Even though he had an exceptional mind that could create the most vivid imaginary situations, he wanted more. He was greedy and believed that by taking away the joy from others he could gain more power for himself.

He did this by transforming himself into a crow that could enter any Gifted Ones imagination with a dark destructive light force stealing their Mindful Gift. The Mindful Watchers were born and soon the founding fathers, fell prey to his dark cult.

Worldwide each district appoints their own leader who are believed to be anointed spiritually by his dark force.

Our leader is Victor Traverse."

Hannah, sat still keeping a straight face, trying to process what she had been told.

"Unlike our white light, theirs is a grey light which transforms them into Watchercrows, watching The Gifted Ones. It's really something to see and the motorbike is my only salvation to escape. My parents must know I lean towards the light of being a Gifted One, but somehow I must be protected.

You're going to ask me about the unicorn keyring, aren't you?" reading Hannah's mind. "It was a gift," he said.

"Gift from whom?" Hannah replied inquisitively.

"An old lady who lives nearby, Mrs Doodle. She's despised among The Watchers as she's Gifted but refuses to leave. Everyone thinks she's a witch, because no-one can detect her Mindful energy. They think she's created a spell to protect herself. You must have walked past her house, it's the one with the fruit grove."

Hannah was piecing it all together, knowing exactly who the old lady was, along with the Watcher leader, Victor.

"What did she say about the keyring?" she asked.

"That my motorbike wasn't my only salvation and that one day if I needed help, I could call upon the unicorn, but only in life or death circumstances."

Hannah slipped her hand into her pocket again to feel for the tiny Book of Spells. It was all beginning to get too much for her and it was now getting late.

"Tom, I think I'd better head off."

The journey back down the mountain was reminiscent of the one with Mini. Both were silent much of the time. Hannah was trying to make sense of it all.

"Thanks Tom," she said as she got off his motorbike, giving him a hug. She felt fond of him and somewhat sorry for him but unable to place all of her emotions.

"So, see you soon?" Tom asked eagerly.

"Yes, of course. I just need time to think about everything Tom."

She needed a plan she thought as she headed home back down Spyglass Hill Drive.

The Book of Spells, the unicorn, Tom's hawk, Victor, it was all whizzing around in her head on the way home.

The air was getting considerably cooler and, in the distance, a low mist hung towards the bottom of the Drive.

In one of the long narrow gardens on the left she could hear raised voices, disagreeable voices with bitter undertones. Knowing no other diversion, she was faced with having to walk past the house. She kept her head hung low.

Out of the sinister silence came a muffled squeal followed by a hiss, and then an evil voice that said, "Come to destroy us have you, Gifted One?"

Hannah screamed.

A few yards ahead, clearly visible, stood the same man she had seen a few days ago. In heavy black jeans, thick sturdy belt, open necked shirt and boots, he wore a leather necklace with a crow pendant that was pulsating on his chest. He threw his head back in rage shouting,

"Never!"

A huge tunnel of grey light burst forth from his chest. Hannah stood rigid, watching his body transform into a crow. Flying first towards her then making a loud caw he flew off into the mist.

Traumatized, Hannah fled as fast as she could towards home, looking over her shoulder every few paces, whilst thinking hard about the burning sun painting, remembering Mini telling her that it could be used as a cry for help.

The warmth of her Grandmother's home drew Hannah in and as she ran up the drive the high, white, double vaulted doors flung open. Falling into Mini's arms, who was standing at the foot of the stairs, she burst into tears.

"Oh, my darling Hannah," Mini said.

Consoling each other they both wept. Suddenly, a miracle occurred and without either of their Gifted imaginations, Parky came to life.

Looking down from the shelf, with his eyes full of unconditional love, he picked up his right paw, the shelf creaked as it always did. Swishing his tail he leapt down, landing on the staircase with a thud, directly behind them. He nestled in between them both and started to chirp, then with his deep, meaningful voice said,

"My burning heart is so full of love for you both and I want you to place your trust in me, to protect you from evil."

They both put their arms around him and resting their heads either side of his body closed their eyes.

They were safe, for now.

'A huge tunnel of grey light burst forth from his chest. Hannah stood rigid, watching his body transform into a crow.'

CHAPTER SEVEN

CREATING A MINDFUL ARMY

Hannah was at her Grandmother's home feeling secure and settled. The comparison between here and Watcherland, that Tom had shared with her earlier, could not have been more different.

In the days that followed much of the time Hannah's Gifted imagination was alive and so too were her imaginary friends. This was time well spent because following her meeting with Tom she knew the day would fast approach when she would have to rely on these friends and the qualities they possessed in her fight against The Mindful Watchers.

In Nancy the lamp she had a good look out. Knowing she had also been faithful to Mini, Nancy spent a lot of her time wobbling and peering through the blinds, tilting her liberty lamp, anxiously looking for potential Watchers. This was very important as they could come at any hour of the day or night. She was like a guard looking out from a fortress.

These precious days also brought along with them lessons.

In the painting of young Mini, Hannah began to learn even more about her Grandmother along with her imaginary pet lion, Duchess. The young Mini would be her valiant right-hand woman, anticipating conflict with The Watchers.

Hannah thought she would entrust Pentheus the leopard to be at the military helm of the battle. Swift and shrewd, as well as polite, he could orchestrate their forces.

Then there were the sun and moon paintings hanging almost opposite each other.

The sun was probably the most powerful of Hannah's and Mini's tools as Hannah knew how blinding it could become, as well as ferociously hot, making it deadly.

The moon hanging above Parky was somewhat of a mystery, but in Hannah's imagination she could make it ten, twenty, even fifty times larger.

The portraits of Bertie and Wallis on the stairs, Mini's swish Godparents were neither Watchers nor Gifted Ones but Naturals. They were good decoys. She'd played Mindfully with them from time to time and thought they could be a good diversion from The Watchers.

It made her wonder about who could be Natural. She began to subconsciously group people she knew in her life, along with her friends and family into this category. Were Naturals completely unaware and unreceptive? Were they innocent and lacked courage to believe?

Tom needed to find the courage to change, and if he could, how many more people might she be able to enlighten into becoming Gifted?

Maybe Tom's lack of trust which she sensed was due to a lack of confidence made him easily led, with an inability to fight his own inner battle with The Watchers.

Like her father a thinker, she silenced the chatter of her mind. She needed to focus and get back to constructing her mindful army.

The owl at the top of the stairs was an interesting old soul. Not as powerful in her mind as some of her other friends, yet useful as he spent many an hour flapping insanely. Nevertheless, he would be another good look out with Nancy and strategically well placed at the top of the stairs by Parky.

Belinda the portrait would be her council, along with Mini, of course. In her mind, Hannah had got her Mindful allies in place and with Parky by her side anything was possible in her quest to defeat The Mindful Watchers.

'Beautiful bedlam' was how Mini described the house when it was entirely ignited by imagination. However, Mini had to regularly remind Hannah to be skilful with her Gift, because when her Mindful energy was at its peak, she was also closer to danger.

It was evening time and the pair were sitting poolside on the swing-boat. The starry night made it feel like a haven and they sat cuddled up to one another, cautious of any Watchercrows close by.

"It was Victor who terrorised you on the way back from Tom's," Mini whispered. "He's anointed spiritually by The Great Gifted Nickolous's dark force and is menacing.

You're a threat because you carry such bright pure energy. They know that you could crush their cult."

Mrs Doodle hadn't come into the conversation yet, not until Hannah thought she would produce the Book of Spells from her pocket.

"Can we go inside Mini? There's something I want to show you."

Seated in another favourite spot at the bottom of the stairs, with Parky looking on, Hannah told Mini all about the old woman and the chaotic weather patterns she had experienced. Mini of course already knew the old woman, this was because Mrs Doodle was her twin sister.

"The chaotic weather phenomenon would have been a test from The Great Star of the Cosmos to see if you were ready for the journey ahead. All will be revealed in due course," Mini said, winking at her.

She felt that whilst Hannah seemed to be lost in her thoughts, that it would be a good time to explain to her the truth.

Mini would have to go back to her youth and her circus days, back to the time Victor fell under the dark force of The Watchers and when she had returned home alone.

Following the tragic loss of their parents, William and Nancy Cernobbio, Mini and Doodle felt a desire to join the travelling Iranian circus, 'The Kamanis Circus.'

Both parents had been returning home from Nancy's Birthday shopping trip to New York, when their aeroplane crashed.

Mini and Doodle temporarily left their parental home to the trust and safe keeping of their new family, Wallis, Bertie and their son Victor.

Victor took the departure of the girls badly and their absence left a void in his life, making him feel excluded.

The three of them had never been encouraged to develop their imaginary powers as the twin's parents never got the chance to nurture their daughters' Gifts before they died and Victors parents being Naturals, were completely devoid of the situation.

So, the girls boldly began their new adventure, discovering and deepening their Gifts.

At times Doodle doubted hers, whilst back at home Victor was seething about his perceived abandonment, whilst harbouring a grudge and creating a hook of negativity for dark powers to latch upon and enter his life.

Whilst at the circus, Mini, the fairer of the twins caught the ringmaster's eye. Before long she was tasked with handling his prized possessions, Parky the panther and Pentheus the leopard.

Doodle's jealousy, that had lay hidden for many years, began the dispute between the girls.

Perceiving she had less than Mini both in her personal relationships and worldly goods, Doodle did not realise that some Gifts granted by The Great Star of the Cosmos may appear more glamorous yet carry a burden of responsibility.

Listening intently, Hannah began to subconsciously consider and compare her own relationship with Amelia.

Mini was revered among her peers at the circus for the bond she had adopted with the big cats, but sadly for Doodle it was all too much, resulting in her feeling inadequate. No matter how hard she tried, she couldn't replicate Mini's imaginative power and bond with them.

Her resentment made her grow bitter and she became cold hearted, just as Victor had.

The spirit of The Great Gifted Nickolous intervened into the gulf of despondency that Doodle and Victor were feeling. The dark power pranced upon it, seizing the opportunity to convert them into Watchers.

Upon doing so other Watchers helped to feed their negativity and misery.

The moment they started to venture on the wrong side of the tracks, they became engrained in the lifestyle and ways of The Watchers.

Sadly, deciding to clutch on to this false security, Doodle never returned home.

Victor's conversion was most dramatic. The dark force had big plans to twist his soul.

Late, on a cold crisp clear night, Victor sat feeling lonely in his father's armchair, staring at the remaining embers from the last log, in the fireplace.

In the silence, above the soft crackling that gripped the room

Victor realised his parents Grandfather clock that stood next to the fireside hadn't chimed. Standing around six-feet-tall the deco styled clock face was supported by six brass pipes either side of the chimes, that hung down the middle.

Walking over to it Victor stared blankly at the clock face. On the hour, it was motionless.

"Chime, come on, chime." he grunted impatiently.

A chill began to fill the air, immediately extinguishing the remaining embers. As smoke began to rise up the chimney, the cream coloured clock face took on a glow turning it a blush pink.

The numerals began to change and soft blue eyes replaced the numbers ten and two, whilst a pleasing wide grin began to form between the eight and the four. It was inviting as well as warming. The brass work gleamed and Victor was surrounded by a warmth that filled the air.

Breaking the silence the clock chimed. Its face had now turned grey and the characteristics had altered. The eyes were dark and narrowed. Black feathers had sprouted, covering the entire face. A pointed beak growing outwards had broken the glass and with an almighty deafening squawk it had transformed into a crow's face.

Victor, terrified, ran out of the house. The ground around him began to quake and crack open and a murderous multitude of crows burst forth.

At that moment a lightening bolt stuck Victor, burning the hair off his head. He had fallen victim to The Great Gifted Nickolous.

All three estranged, Mini never saw Victor again and had heard over the years that Doodle's heart had softened and she became humble. She had reconciled the past with herself and her heart began to radiate a bright light once again. The Great Star of the Cosmos was so pleased with her that she was granted 'tools' to use to help overcome the forces of evil that had once trapped her. This was on the condition that she lived and would abide among The Watchers in the hope of converting them to the light as well.

"So now you understand more about Victor and you also know about Doodle, her fruit grove and why her home radiates warmth. Her gift is valuable, keep it safe Hannah." Mini said, feeling exhausted and emotional having told the story.

Hannah kept the Book of Spells safely under her pillow at night and in her pocket by day. Settling down into bed that very night her energy began to stir.

Belinda the portrait was coming to life and as usual appearing in a cloudy haze, hovering above her bed.

"My dear Hannah, things are difficult for Tom right now. Trouble is brewing among the Watchers. A storm is coming, and you must learn to harness your Gift and learn to act as well as respond to what's coming."

Belinda lifted both hands, covering her face exposing beautiful red nails. She then laid them flat in front of Hannah, palms facing upwards revealing the hologram of a tornado whistling and turning. Suddenly she snapped the image shut between her palms, to the sound of crows cawing.

"Believe in your Gift and continue to love with an open heart." She was then sucked away in a haze.

Hannah buried her head into the pillows, trying to sleep and trying hard not to think about what Mini as well as Belinda had just told her.

Morning came and the daylight outside sneaked through the bedroom shutters. The sun cast a ray of light upon Belinda and recalling her words from the night before Hannah felt gloom deepen within her.

It was without a skip and a jump that morning that she ventured out of her bedroom to greet Mini for breakfast.

Times were certainly changing again, and this wasn't going to be a normal day, not that any day was ever normal at Mini's, because waiting at the bottom of the stairs with Mini was Tom.

'Breaking the silence the clock chimed. Black feathers had sprouted, covering the entire face and a pointed beak broke through the glass.'

CHAPTER EIGHT

THE GREAT STAR OF THE COSMOS

Hannah's heart leapt momentarily as she saw Tom standing with Mini at the bottom of the stairs. She was fond of Tom, but when she saw him, she felt defensive and she couldn't understand why. His face, the colour of alabaster, made his eyes appear darker and his wavy hair was tousled from wearing his motorbike helmet.

Hannah walked slowly down the wooden sweeping staircase trying to fathom out what was happening. There was a sense of angst in the air.

"Let's make tea!" Mini said, clapping her hands together trying to normalise the situation.

"Boy, am I in trouble, Hannah. We need to talk," Tom said.

Hannah, raising her eyebrows, acknowledged what he'd said and made her way to the kitchen. Tom, however, decided to linger in the hallway with his arms folded staring pensively at Parky upon the shelf.

"Tom!" Mini yelled, "tea's ready."

Following her shrill tones, Tom found them both in the kitchen, Hannah perched on a stool while Mini dashed around arranging cups and saucers at her usual speed.

"The battle for minds and hearts has begun," Mini said, sighing and shaking her head whilst pouring the tea.

"Yeah, the cult is getting bigger and bigger every day!" Tom affirmed.

"Ever since your visit, Victor has been on the war path calling more Mindful Watchers to join him and stop your crusade! The good news is Mrs. Doodle is brighter than ever and there are rumours she has converted some of The Watchers to the light, but the other Watchers are coming for you and," he paused.

"And what?" Mini asked.

Tom looked down and drank his tea avoiding the question.

Hannah anxiously put her head down into her hands, thinking. So, this is what Belinda the portrait was insinuating when she said 'trouble.'

"Is there anything you can tell us Tom, to help us, anything?"

Tom hung his head. Hannah felt he was hiding something from her.

"Look, I shouldn't be here, my parents said they would take my motorbike from me and look, I've got to go."

Feeling a terrible sense of guilt for engaging in any kind of discussion with Hannah and Mini, Tom was trying desperately to be brave in his fight against The Watchers. The pressure from his parents was weighing heavy. Watcher betrayal came at a high price.

It was well known that the punishment for being a disloyal Watcher was to be permanently transformed into a crow. This was something that only the leaders of the council had the authority to do.

An eternity as a Watchercrow was both a barbaric and terrifying prospect. Enslaved to the darkness; it was a cruel act to bestow upon their own kind.

On the occasions that Tom had met Victor he had displayed an uncharacteristic softness towards him. He hoped that Victor might be merciful towards him.

Hannah walked with Tom to the high, white, double vaulted doors, but he stopped and taking a deep breath looked up at Parky.

"You are so lucky to live in the light, Hannah."

Feeling sorry for him, she said, "We can work this out together, Tom. Why don't I come over to your place and we can visit Mrs. Doodle and see if she can help us."

"We could try," he said fretting, raising his eyebrows, and half smiling.

They arranged what they thought was a safe time to go the next day. Then out of the blue Tom randomly blurted, "Why don't you come on the panther?" Hannah glanced up at Parky, thinking that was probably not a bad idea.

The sound of Tom's motorbike could be heard for quite a few

moments after he'd left, and sitting at the bottom of the staircase Hannah held her head in her hands thinking. Mini tiptoed over and, sitting beside her, gently put an arm around her, "Our minds are becoming a warzone, aren't they?" she said.

The rest of the day the pair, deep in thought, pottered around the house. From time to time Hannah would reach into her pocket for the Book of Spells, mainly as a kind of reassurance more than anything else. She also spent a great deal of time thinking and planning for a potential attack by The Watchers, but most of all wondered if she should visit Mrs Doodle with Tom. She wondered what Mini felt about them visiting her twin sister.

At the end of another emotionally charged day, Hannah placed the Book of Spells under her pillow and quickly drifted off into a familiar deep dream.

A bright refracted light filled the room forming a rainbow. Dark thunderous clouds loomed beyond it. Once again at the top of the arch was Parky, but unlike before, he wasn't beckoning Hannah with his paw. Instead he was standing still with sorrowful eyes. Behind him stood Mrs Doodle, in her red hooded cape.

Above her head she was holding an orange, picked from the grove. Tenderly, presenting the fruit before him she pierced it with a knife, squirting the juice over his head.

He humbly stood still as the juice dripped down his face and he licked his mouth in a despondent fashion. Collapsing, he slid down the rainbow lifelessly into the darkness.

Mrs Doodle lowering the hood of her cape revealed the face of Victor, head tilted back, roaring with laughter.

When Hannah recited her dream the next morning, the intensity of the situation with The Watchers suddenly struck Mini. She understood from the dream that danger was imminent and, concerned for Doodle as well as Hannah, suggested that perhaps she went along to meet Tom and hopefully Doodle instead.

"Mini, I can do this, please let me go."

She knew she would have to let Hannah go and spread her own wings. At least she would be with her trusted imaginary friend Parky, Mini thought.

It was decided, Hannah would enlighten her imagination and take Parky to meet Tom and hopefully Doodle.

"Be humble Hannah, it will lead you to the truth," Mini said.

Nervously, with a half proud smile, Hannah peered up at Parky. It was as if she was going into battle and he was her war horse, except this was a different kind of battle, a battle of belief.

It was daytime and the sun was shining brightly through the square window in front of the chandelier. The extreme intensity of the light upon Parky's copper coat crystallized into millions of sparkles. Hannah's imagination was coming to life and as it did Parky moaned, turning his head, raising his left paw and the shelf creaked as it always did.

Glancing over at Hannah his heart leapt in love for her and he sprung off the shelf landing at the bottom of the staircase. Knowing she was loved by Parky, Hannah felt a freedom to love others, even The Mindful Watchers.

Narrowing his eyes, in a deep and meaningful voice he said,

"Hold on tight Hannah and always remember, *only if you believe can you make the impossible, possible*," reminding her of her Gifted obligations.

He then nudged her legs and she toppled onto his back.

Thrusting his chest forward, he once again sprouted the most beautiful thick white lustrous wings, transforming into a winged panther. Hannah bent forward reaching ahead of his wings to grab his neck, but before she had a chance she was pushed back by his speed and all at once they were flying.

Parky ascended swiftly and with his huge gigantic wings made long large clapping sounds as they flapped, reaching altitude.

It was extremely cold and a silence hung in the air. Parky was keeping a safe distance so The Mindful Watchers would not be able to detect Hannah's Mindful energy too quickly. He would swoop down directly over Doodle's house, as he thought they would be safe there.

The sky at first was clear, the colour of topaz, then it suddenly went dark, night time dark, the colour of midnight blue and Hannah leant towards Parky's head in fear, wrapping her arms around his neck.

"Look ahead, Hannah," he said.

Ahead of them shone the brightest star, it was long and narrow and its rays seemed to spread far and wide, almost reaching the earth. The centre of it pulsated.

Hannah began to feel entranced and it appeared Parky was as well. He seemed to be flying on autopilot and his wings went limp.

They floated towards the gentle bright force with glazed expressions.

They were much lower now and, returning back from their blissful state, Hannah could see that they were hovering above The Mindful Watchers' homes. The finial tops and pointed turrets of the houses looked like a bed of nails from the sky.

The star, which was The Great Star of the Cosmos, shone over one particular house, Mrs Doodle's, as a warning of where evil forces lay. A warning Hannah did not understand.

'Ahead of them shone the brightest star, it was long and narrow and its rays seemed
to spread far and wide, almost reaching the earth.'

CHAPTER NINE

THE CROW TORNADO

Approaching Mrs Doodle's, Parky's eye's narrowed, it was Watchers weather, cold and damp.

Full of Mindful energy in the heart of Watcherland Hannah felt in terrible danger. She checked her pocket for the Book of Spells, as Parky landed with a thud.

They had arrived in Mrs Doodle's long thin garden and a deadly silence cut through the air.

Quietly dismounting Parky, lying strewn on the damp pavers, she noticed Tom's motorbike, as if abandoned. Dangling from the handlebars the unicorn keyring had changed to a dark grey colour.

The grove was abundant, fruit that had fallen was scattered everywhere. Seeing an orange lying by the motorbike and feeling thirsty Hannah picked it up and peeling back some of the skin squeezed it into her mouth.

Within seconds the trees were bending in a rubber like fashion and the grass had grown up to her knees. Staggering to the pathway, which now resembled a slithering snake, Hannah wobbled as if hypnotized towards Mrs Doodle's front door.

"Hannah, stay focused. I have the power to remain in your imagination," Parky said in a low voice, standing behind her.

Hannah, squinting at him, noticed his head was larger than his body. Looking into his doe-eyed gaze she could see the reflection of a red hooded cape; it was Mrs Doodle's.

As Hannah became fully aware again, she turned around and under one of the fruit trees there the cape lay. The experience had delayed her from getting into the house and confused she began to wonder where Tom was.

She reached for the brass door knocker, shaped like a panther's head, and as she did it the Book of Spells slipped out of her pocket and a gust of wind blew it down the pathway.

"Hannah," Parky said in an urgent deep whisper, "The energy from your Mindful Gift is stirring The Watchers."

Several Watchercrows were now circling above and she was sensing impending danger. Once inside Mrs Doodle's house they would be safe she thought, knocking on the door.

As it opened slowly, a warm inviting light flowed out.

Just as Hannah was about to step inside, she was distracted as a voice from the direction of the grove called out to her.

"I'm sorry Hannah, I really am," it was Tom.

Mrs Doodle's door instantly slammed shut and remnants of the light inside flowed under the door onto the pathway.

Hannah bent down and peering forward she could see it was Tom.

"Oh Tom!" she said with relief. "Quickly, come here," gesturing him over.

"No Hannah, I can't, it's over," A tear ran down his pale face.

"This is a hoax Hannah, he's betrayed you," Parky whispered in her ear. "We must go, now!"

There was an urgency in his voice and he nudged her legs with his head and she toppled onto his back. Thoughts began pounding through Hannah's head and for a moment or two she sat on Parky's back frozen, not knowing who or what to believe.

Tom had no intention of joining her to meet Mrs Doodle she thought rationally, and this was clearly a trap to bring her and Parky to The Watchers.

In awe of Parky's magnificence, Tom stood speechless as he watched him prowling with Hannah on his back.

"Tom, you lied to me! You deliberately kept me outside with Parky for as long as possible so that The Watchers could detect my energy, didn't you? How could you! I thought you were on our side; I thought you wanted to do this together."

Tom, already nervous, was feeling extremely intimidated by Parky's size and stature.

"Hannah, you don't understand. I was blackmailed, I had no choice. The Watchers are so angry with us…I'm so sorry."

Parky, saddened to hear Tom's confession, hissed and jumped Mrs Doodle's gate, landing on Spyglass Hill Drive. He moaned and hissed again, then narrowing his eyes he puffed his lean chest forward. He was preparing for a flight of survival and began sprouting his wings. He then quickly tucked them in tightly, composing himself in preparation to run.

A little down the hill were a full gang of Watchers. There they stood, all ages, arms folded in defiance as the spectacle unfolded. They were dressed in their usual uniform of black; men in belted heavy jeans with shirts and boots, women in long gypsy style skirts, ankle boots and blouses. Some of the children, dressed in a similar fashion, timidly hung onto their parent's legs, whilst others were running wild. Their small feet could be heard tapping through the water as they squelched through puddles at speed.

Many of the adults began to transform into Watchercrows through the grey tunnel of light pouring out of their chests. In the process of doing so they were tilting their heads back and crying out in anger,

"Never!"

"What do you want with us Gifted One?"

It was terrifying. The pale skinned children abruptly stopping, stood mouths agape as their parents transformed.

Parky grew in stature again and was now five times larger than his original size, dwarfing The Watchers. His copper fur coat sparkled, and his white lustrous wings were spellbinding against the dark facade of the area. His presence for some of The Watchers was blinding, as he bore such great light.

Frightened, they crossed their arms over their faces in his shadow. Others cowardly took a few steps back. The Watchers were closer than ever to cruelly destroying Parky from Hannah's imagination forever. The only option for escape was for Parky to make a swift, short run and an almost vertical ascent into flight, gaining distance as soon as possible with his almighty wings.

The Watchers were now gaining in number as they came out of their long thin gardens onto the street. Hannah sat holding tightly onto Parky, looking around in fear. She could see Tom mount his motorbike and speed away. Seconds seemed like minutes and she knew time was running out.

"Parky home, home Parky now!" she said, leaning forward shouting into his ear.

She closed her eyes as she knew she was about to be thrust backwards, then upwards at great speed. She Mindfully thought about the burning sun painting, desperately hoping Mini was as well.

Parky moaned as he ascended. It was hard work and he struggled through the now bracing winds. Once they had levelled out, Hannah looked over her shoulder. The intensity of Hannah's imagination combined with the power of Parky had stirred a Mindful energy unlike any other.

Behind them, dark clouds were forming and a long thin tunnel of cloud emerged. It was a tornado and Watchercrows were being drawn into it as it was moving in the direction of where they were flying.

Resembling a cone of dark feathers it twisted itself over the landscape in a dark dance. The shrill sound of twisted wind and broken glass filled the sky. This was a Watchercrow tornado and closing in on Parky, struggling to keep up speed and strength.

"Faster Parky, faster," Hannah urged him on. He dipped his head to gain extra speed, then soared.

Some of Watchercrows had broken away from the tornado being tossed in the air like puppets.

All the time Hannah was trying to keep her mind on the burning sun but fear was choking her belief in her Gift.

The tornado began to resemble the face of Victor and mouthed, "Never!"

It was too much for Hannah and her Gifted energy shifted. Parky suddenly disappeared but remarkably she was still flying, as a bird, a raven. She could see her jet black long pointed beak in front of her, and to the sides her long tapered wings cut through the air like rigid pieces of expertly cut black silk. It felt absurd yet natural.

Camouflaged, into what was now dusk, she felt protected as she steered herself. Looking backwards, the tornado was dying down and she could see Mini's house in the distance. Flames were sprouting from the windows from the burning sun painting, defending, protecting.

Mini stood in front of the high, white, double vaulted doors peering up into the early night sky. The scene was apocalyptic.

As Hannah landed, she looked Mini in the eye, shook herself and walked out of her bird-like state into her arms. She was home again. Parky was on the shelf but the Book of Spells was missing.

'Behind them, dark clouds were forming, and a long thin tunnel of cloud emerged. It was a tornado and the crows were being drawn into it.'

CHAPTER TEN

THE ARRIVAL OF THE SPIRITS

Hannah, traumatized by the recent events, licked her wounds as she longed for home in the little market town of Ash-by-by-the-Sea which seemed a million miles away. She strangely missed her twin Amelia and wanted to share with her the experiences she'd had. She wondered, yet again if she too might be Mindfully Gifted, in the knowledge that both Mini and Mrs Doodle were.

The onset of homesickness combined with the uncertainty of what lay ahead only fuelled her desire to complete her quest. Little things she recalled when she'd flown back to Mini's began to occupy her mind. The bright star and the number of stars cluttered above Mini's house, the flames which had sprouted through the windows from the burning sun painting. Then there was her transformation to a raven and Parky disappearing.

This was truly the greatest Gift on earth, her imagination could come to life, but where did it come from and why?

Many questions lay unanswered and she only had a patchy recollection of the visit to meet Tom at Mrs Doodle's. What she did recall though was Mrs Doodle's cape and of course the missing Book of Spells.

It was evening time and instead of sitting poolside on the swing boat for their regular chat, Grandmother and Granddaughter sat snuggled up in Hannah's bed, both with their arms folded on top of the sheets. Mini in red silk and Hannah in checked pyjama sets.

"Mini, can you please tell me about The Great Star of the Cosmos? I think Parky and I saw it."

"What did you see?" Mini asked.

"The most beautiful star ever," Hannah recalled, tilting her head back dreamily, "it was a long narrow star with rays that spread as far wide as long, almost reaching the earth. Parky and I were drawn to it uncontrollably and it shone directly above Mrs Doodle's house."

"Well, Hannah, The Great Star of the Cosmos, is the progenitor of the universe, granting us Gifts. It yields goodness, protects and promotes love. *It shines upon those who shine.*

Then taking a deep breath in and sighing, Mini asked, "Did you see Doodle at all?"

"Only her red cape, reflected in Parky's eyes," replied Hannah.

"We need to trust in The Great Star that all will be revealed," Mini said, kissing the top of Hannah's head.

"Trusting is as important as believing. The Star works in mysterious ways- we must always trust that no matter what situation it puts us in, it is what is meant to be. Remember, flying as a raven protected you as you fell from your imaginative Gift."

In keeping with their conversation, as though she'd been eavesdropping somehow, Hannah's imaginary friend, Belinda, peering down at them both, said in her usual smoky voice, "Those who have true belief carry brightness wherever they go."

Hannah's imagination had momentarily come to life, lighting up the entire room.

Peace remained in the house for the rest of the evening, however, the very next day this was to be replaced with sadness. Astounded, Hannah witnessed even more grief and sorrow for her grandmother. How much sadness could one person carry in their lifetime.

Waking bleary eyed, Hannah made her way down the sweeping staircase. Mini was in the hallway kneeling in front of the high, white, double vaulted doors, crouched over in tears.

"What's wrong?" Hannah said consoling her.

Nursing Doodle's neatly folded red cape on her knee, Mini, hands shaking, clearly in a state of shock, held a handwritten note in gold pen, it read,

> *To my Dearest Sister, Mini,*
> *You know I have battled living among The Watch-*
> *ers, yet I've been aided graciously by The Great Star of*

the Cosmos.

It's true, I have found happiness along my way. My heart's healed and the light from my good work abounds.

However, The Great Star has called me and in body I shall no longer here abide.

In celebration of my good works and life, I have been granted three Spirits to send forth to you, to help you and Hannah in your battle in the quest against The Watchers.

They are named, Faith, Hope and Charity, they will arrive soon and dwell among you.

Until we meet again sweet sister. Doodle

Consumed in grief for the rest of the day, haunted by past memories of loved ones lost, it was a welcome relief for Mini that the Spirits did arrive that very evening in the form of shooting stars, defying the atmosphere. There were flashes of lightning and great turbulence that shook the house.

Hannah and Mini stood in front of the high, white, double vaulted doors observing the spectacle, unafraid of their visitors' approach. Wind blew through their hair and clothing, rippling their faces.

The Spirits held a potent force and along with it protection. They danced and swayed through the night sky down towards Mini and Hannah and when they arrived the wind ceased.

They had heads the size of a football, resembling jellyfish, with translucent glowing tails. They were the most unusual specimens ever to be seen.

In turn, each came face to face with Mini and Hannah, mirroring their image whilst making high pitched giggling sounds at the same time. Then they carelessly floated into the house bringing it to life.

Mini and Hannah could feel their own light being awakened but it wasn't needed. The Spirits came with the power to aid The Gifted Ones. The house, as Mini had described before, was once again returning to 'beautiful bedlam'.

Parky began pacing on the spot upon the shelf, lifting his front and rear legs simultaneously. He then jumped majestically down onto the black and white tiled hall floor. Standing still he looked around, happiness oozing from his eyes.

Nancy the lamp, instead of wobbling, worrying and peering out for The Watchers now shone her liberty lamp with confidence.

Even Pentheus the leopard with all his pride and valour couldn't hide his joy as he strolled around trying to contain himself. Relenting, he rolled onto his back and played with Duchess the lion, as the painting of young Mini had come to life.

The young Mini was performing a playful warrior's dance, waving her sword above her head.

Hannah and Mini greedily feasted on the extravagance. It was like an imaginative Mardi Gras and they happily joined in the fun. It certainly gave Mini momentary relief from her grief. She knew that The Great Star would never burden her with more than she could handle. She was a woman of admirable strength.

The sun painting was shooting flames whilst the moon painting developed a bright happy face watching over the jollities.

Looking around, the owl that sat on the top of the stairs whooshed by.

It was all happening, even Bertie and Wallis leapt out of their frames, waltzing together at the top of the stairs.

Belinda the portrait suddenly appeared like a genie of the lamp from underneath the bedroom door. Swelling in size she hovered in the air over the festivities.

All was content in the house for now and the hurt from Tom's betrayal of Hannah had temporarily subsided.

*'Nursing Doodle's neatly folded red cape on her knee, Mini, hands shaking, held a
handwritten note in gold pen.'*

CHAPTER ELEVEN

TOM'S UNICORN

The joyous scene inside Mini's wasn't quite the same outside. Anxiety amongst The Mindful Watchers had accelerated. The Spirits arrival had increased their existing anger, fuelling dark clouds and rumbling thunder. Many had permanently transformed into Watchercrows, circling whilst watching Mini's home like never before, or patiently waiting perched in palm trees.

A different breed of Watcher from further afield sat among the flock, an enhanced raven species. Their eyes had cameras, able to record everything they saw in ultra- high definition. Information was stored so that when they transformed back into Watchers, they were able to replay and watch what they had recorded. They were called, Cawcams.

It was yet another obstacle in Hannah's quest and she didn't even know they existed. However, Tom did, but he was consumed with guilt for enticing Hannah to bring Parky to Mrs Doodle's. What help could he be now?

Distraught, he was a broken young man who felt all his dreams and chances of reform were dashed after he had betrayed his only hope.

Loyalty to The Great Gifted Nickolous was entrenched in every Watchers soul, making them subservient. They were becoming increasingly pleased with the friendship forming between Hannah and Tom, knowing that their closeness was the connection to Parky they needed. When their chance came they would seize the panther once and for all, destroying him for eternity.

They had been watching the young couple since Tom had taken Hannah flying up into the mountains.

Hannah had shrewdly noticed them as well. It was the very same night that Tom's parents had blackmailed him, demanding a cruel ultimatum. It was beginning to crush Margaret and Richard Keys. Their love for Tom was greater than any for the Crowcode but Margaret and Richard were wavering. Their allegiance to Victor and The Great Gifted Nickolous was all consuming and the urge to trap Hannah with Parky was their ultimate act of loyalty towards them.

It was all coming together in Tom's confused mind as he sat alone in despair at home under the porch. Fiddling with the unicorn keyring, which was now grey in colour having lost its sparkle, he reached into his pocket to retrieve the tiny, red, leather-bound Book of Spells.

Quickly looking around to check no one was about he held it in the palm of his hand. He recalled the moment he had picked it up from Mrs Doodle's path when the gust of wind had blown it away from Hannah. It must be hers or Mrs Doodle's he thought.

However, news from the Cawcams was out that Mrs Doodle was dead. If it was Hannah's, how was he going to return it to her now? Would she ever forgive him? Tears ran down his pale face.

Pandemonium was breaking out amongst The Watchers. More than ever he was feeling alienated from both family and friends, with no hope of reaching her.

"Keep the faith," he whispered to his inner self, lowering his head as his tears fell upon both the unicorn and the Book of Spells.

With each tear drop the unicorn began to sparkle more and the golden clasp on the Book of Spells began to twitch.

Fear, not sorrow, began to suddenly grip him and he nervously looked around again, checking no-one was about. Then, crouching behind his motorbike, he slowly and carefully opened the golden clasp. The tiny papyrus pages were blank, but each new tear began to form a letter, then a word and finally a sentence, with instructions that read,

Return me to Hannah under the coat of The Watchers, upon the gift I gave you.

Snapping the book to, shocked and placing it in the top right-hand pocket of his leather jacket, he shivered and got onto his motorbike, slumping over the handlebars. It seemed days since he'd taken his motorbike up into the Bretalina mountains. All he wanted to do now was to escape and take time to think about how he was going to go about it all.

He looked around. The sky was dark and the air had grown extremely damp. A smell similar to mould filled the air. The black clouds had brought heavy rain and with it thunder cracked loudly. The rain poured like a waterfall off the porch roof onto the street.

Tom closed his eyes and with a heavy heart sighed. Opening them he could see Watchers in a daze roaming around, waiting for further instruction. These would come in either the form of a loud cawing siren, from The Spectacle council headquarters itself, or via tiny public address systems, carried in the Watchercrows claws.

The women's black gypsy skirts dragged in the puddles, whilst the majority of the children now staggered alongside, holding tightly onto their legs. The men, in their usual attire had their shirt sleeves rolled up and were huddled together in groups, arms folded, ready to seize control. Occasionally some of the men would walk away from the group, arch their backs and thrust their chests forward, projecting huge tunnels of grey light, transforming into Watchercrows. The scene was so frightening.

Tom slapped the side of his head several times and wiped away the tears with the back of his hand, "Think, come on, think. What does it mean?" he said aloud to himself desperately.Return me to Hannah under the coat of The Watchers, upon the gift I gave you.

He went over the instruction in his head several times. "But upon what gift?"

Thoughts raced around his head as he sat on his motorbike

fiddling with the unicorn. Time was passing and he felt a sense of urgency to unravel the riddle.

Suddenly it all became clear.

The gift was the unicorn keyring from Mrs Doodle. He remembered the day she had presented it to him from under her red cape.

Reassuringly she had told him that his motorbike wasn't his only salvation and that the keyring could be called upon if he needed it, but only in life or death circumstances.

Tom started to gain strength and hope. He would have to bring the unicorn to life using his Mindful Gift and trust it would take him to Hannah.

Meanwhile, the atmosphere at Mini's had become solemn and apprehension hung in the air. It was very much a case of preparing for a 'battle of the minds' as Mini had once described it.

The house was very much aware of The Watchers' presence and on full alert. Mini and Hannah were now so attuned to their Gifts that much of their waking time was spent preparing and rehearsing, should an imminent threat transpire.

The Spirits dwelt among them as Doodle said they would. Mini, still dealing with her grief, felt a huge sense of comfort and gratitude for them and thanks was given daily to the ever all-knowing Great Star of the Cosmos, for love and support. Unbeknown to Mini and Hannah, The Great Star had also decided to paint the night sky with various constellations that would one day work in favour of The Gifted Ones.

Parky knew what was looming and carried a forlorn expression.

His position on the shelf had changed, instead of standing proud with his jaw open baring his teeth, eyes soft, he had moved into a lying position, head resting low on his paws. Hannah pondered Parky's new position with unease as she passed him by on the stairs, as her imaginary power hadn't imagined this.

It would be Belinda who which would reveal the real reason for his change in character. As it had many times before, Hannah's imagination leapt to life. The huge tunnel of light sprung from her chest unveiling a sombre Belinda with a rainbow framing her head.

"Belinda, you seem different," she said, kneeling on her bed looking up to the portrait.

Belinda raised her eyebrows and without a reply looked up towards the rainbow hovering above her. Suddenly black crows emerged one by one from behind the rainbow, then a few more and before long ten, twenty and more were flying above Hannah. She ducked as they swooped through the air above her bed.

"Many will come, it has to be this way," Belinda said, sorrowfully lowering her head. She had swelled in size, almost covering the room, trying to swamp out the birds but still they came. Hannah slipped underneath the sheets, frightened, as Belinda clapped her hands together and the birds vanished. Except for one.

A huge bird with large talons appeared from over the rainbow, carrying a big cat by its shoulders. Peering over the sheets Hannah recognised it as Parky and outstretching her arms towards him shouting, "Noooo!"

The rainbow faded and Belinda was instantaneously sucked back into the portrait.

The bedroom door thrust open. It was Mini. Hannah jumped off the bed sobbing and ran over to her,

"It's The Watchers, Mini. They are coming for Parky."

'It was all coming together in his confused mind as he sat alone in despair, fiddling with the unicorn keyring.'

CHAPTER TWELVE

THE SPECTACLE COUNCIL

Victor had raised a considerable crow army and The Watchers were ready.

The Spectacle council had been sitting for several days. The building where they convened, towards the top end of Spy Glass Hill Drive, was reminiscent of an old air raid shelter and distinguishable by a pair of enormous, round rimmed spectacles that hung adjacent to the entrance.

Inside the main room of the building, long, thin, black benches filled the space leading up to an altar, heavily decorated with black thick feathers. A lectern with the head of a crow stood to the left and hanging above it was an enormous picture of a CrowMan - half crow, half man. Underneath were inscribed the words, 'The Great Gifted Nickolous'.

In the middle of the room, steps led down to a clover leaf

crypt, supported by three pillars. The main chamber was damp and smelled musty.

It was a most sacred place for Watchers, as it was here that Nickolous, the ultimate peer of the dark realm, had chosen to entrust his death mask which was kept inside a glass box upon a stone alter positioned in the middle of the chamber. It was a black mask shaped like a crow's head, with a long black beak pointing upwards.

It was an enormous privilege for this council to host the artefact, which centuries ago had been worn by him, following his death. Whilst lying in state in an open topped copper casket. It was a mystery, where exactly he had finally been laid to rest, but early founding fathers believed it was in a European medieval castle and throughout the ages various relics of his had been preserved and distributed. Watchers today still believed his spirit would have selectively chosen these.

It was the duty of the council to provide Watcherguards, to guard the mask. Standing at the top of the crypt steps, they wore simple white tunics made of muslin with the emblem of a crow in the middle. Intermittently they would transform into Watchercrows and fly around the relic, venerating it. Myth was that these Watchercrows laid their eggs in the crypt.

The council sat in order of rank on the long thin benches and each wore a layer of feathers around their necks at the meetings.

They had finally concluded at their recent meeting that without a doubt the size of their army was considerable enough for a victory, and that their main purpose of attack was to crush Hannah's power, followed by Mini's. The ultimate prize was Parky.

As an act of worship to The Great Gifted Nickolous, local vigils proposed at meetings and approved by Victor, the Leader, had already commenced.

Watchers were burning relics of objects that had once ignited their imaginations from when they were Gifted and truly believed. The bonfires, in the long narrow gardens in front of their homes, produced a range of colour in the flames that were a welcome sight for Tom as they lit the darkness and warmed the cold damp air.

Rocking horses, swings, dolls, pictures, all once meaningful possessions and valued imaginary friends, were now being tossed onto the flames, like scraps to a dog.

Tom nervously lifted up the collar of his leather jacket, and sweeping back his wavy hair he tried hard to fit in with the crowd. The rain had ceased for now and he mingled with some of The Watchers around one of the bonfires.

"Has anyone seen Victor?" he said, in a deep voice, narrowing his eyes.

"Over at that vigil," the woman said, pointing to a house across the street. She gave Tom a double glance.

"Eh, aren't you that kid who's friends with that bright Gifted One?"

"I don't know who you're talking about." He replied, keeping his head down as he scuttled off.

"Eh, come back," the woman called out. "It's him, you know." She started gossiping and telling other Watchers drawing attention to him. Tom could hear a commotion kicking off as he hurriedly walked away.

His heart was beating so fast it was as though his entire body had become a walking heartbeat.

Tom had bravely decided to try and win Victor's confidence. If all worked out, he would be invited to join the crow army and then bring the unicorn to life. It was the only way.

The pendant of the crow on Victor's necklace throbbed. "It came from Doodle?" Victor asked, inquisitively.

"Yes," said Tom, with his hands in his pockets feeling for the unicorn. Thank goodness he had put the Book of Spells in his top right-hand pocket.

"It's here," he said, stuttering, presenting the unicorn. It certainly wasn't vibrant now and the colour had grown darker.

Victor held it in the palm of his hand. For a moment, his gaze softened and looking at Tom, his small dark eyes displayed an aching empathy. Then, snatching the look back the perverse gentleness vanished and tilting his head backwards he roared with laughter. Then with his small, black, piercing eyes he looked directly at Tom and said, "You can join us, we leave tonight."

Thrusting the unicorn keyring back into Tom's hand he walked away in a heavy lopsided manner. Looking down, Tom noticed the unicorn had completely changed colour, it was now black.

Burdened with his forthcoming responsibility he reluctantly joined the crow army.

The vast throng of Watchers had transformed into Watchercrows, occupying many of the streets, with Victor at the helm. Tom, thankfully, felt relatively unnoticed.

The sound of a million feathers flapping rippled through the air causing a dusty wet wind. Commanding the crowd, Victor shouted, "It's time to take control, to crush the curse of The Gifted Ones."

Turning his back to Tom he raised his arms above his head shouting, "Destroy them!"

A dozen or more Watchercrows landed on each of his outstretched arms. "Watch this," he said, looking back at Tom, with eyes of pure evil, "this is real power!"

A dark grey light spurted from his chest as he transformed into a gigantic raven. Tom closed his eyes in disgust. It was a sickening sight to see, even though he had seen it so many times.

Suddenly the Book of Spells began to twitch in his pocket and amidst the sound of feathers flapping he heard a voice, *"Return me to Hannah under the control of The Watchers, upon the gift I gave you."*

Jumping out of Tom's hand the unicorn instantaneously began to grow. He had been saved the humiliation of using his Mindful Gift in front of The Watchers.

Full sized, the winged unicorn stood in front of him, with a jet-black body, resembling a thoroughbred racehorse.

A long wavy mane reached its shoulders, with a tail that almost touched the ground. With wings that were thick, with a relatively short span, the hot blooded unicorn foamed at the mouth, snorting and stomping.

Walking towards Tom, it lowered its head and poked him in the chest, with its incredibly long horn, then raising its head stared directly into Tom's eyes. With a sorrowful look a tear mounted in the corner of its eye. In a peculiar way it reminded Tom of Victor's earlier gaze as well as his own tears upon the Book of Spells.

The unicorn bent its two front legs to allow Tom to mount, then pranced over to Victor who had just taken flight.

Breaking into a canter and gallop the unicorn followed suit and they were soon airborne.

In the damp misty air, the Watchercrows began to get into formation and before long the dampness dropped and they were all soaring. It was much clearer now and the night sky was very dark, the stars were few and far between. The only stars shining brightly were those ahead in the distance, towards where The Gifted Ones lived.

Glancing around, Tom could see that the sky behind him was thick with feathers and beaks. It was as though an enormous black feathered carpet was moving slowly through the night sky. To his left and right the Watchercrows littered the sky as far as the eye could see and all the time a rapid clapping and flapping noise whooshed by.

Tom held tightly onto the unicorn's long black mane, wrapping its hair around one of his wrists, whilst his other hand tapped his top pocket feeling for the Book of Spells. He was finally on his way to Hannah and hoped this tiny book would save them both.

The Spirits dwelling at Mini's were very much aware of the forthcoming attack by The Watchers. They were also aware of the fear and vulnerability that both Hannah and Mini were feeling. They were floating around the house like jelly fish in the sea, singing and praising The Great Star of the Cosmos. The sound was angelic.

Pausing in front of Hannah and Mini who were standing in the kitchen, their singing turned into a series of high- pitched giggles. Blowing strength and confidence onto Mini and Hannah, the heads of the Spirits turned a dazzling white.

Grandmother and Granddaughter fully believing, were now at the pinnacle of Mindful Gift. From now on when their imaginary power came to life the light from their chests would be dazzling white, representing the purity of it.

Even though the house was unsure of what the forthcoming eventualities would be, it emanated warmth, and hand in hand Mini and Hannah began to bring the house to life.

'The building was reminiscent of an old air raid shelter and distinguishable by a pair of enormous, round rimmed spectacles that hung adjacent to the entrance.'

CHAPTER THIRTEEN

PARKY'S TIME

Victor, with his wide arched bill, headed the formation into battle and, releasing a deafening squawk revealed its red raw lining. The situation had exacerbated his anger and frustration to get the job done.

In the distance, the promised constellations designed by The Great Star of the Cosmos many moons ago now littered the sky. The Watchercrows looked on in fearful wonderment trying to make out the formations as they approached.

The first was an outline of a hooded cape, the second of Parky and the third of Pentheus.

There was much squawking to be heard as The Watchercrows made out the shapes.

The cape constellation swished through the sky whilst the ones of the two big cats revealed fierce faces baring teeth and claws, with arched backs and hissing mouths.

As the constellations moved, anguish further gripped the Watchercrows. The weakest simply dropped out of the sky, fearful that the cape signified the return of Mrs Doodle's supposed witchcraft, whilst others were petrified by the power of the big cats.

The wind whistled through Tom's hair as he sat upright on the unicorn also in wonder at the galactic show. An overriding sense of gratitude came over him. This was proof, he thought, that The Gifted were ready to fight back. For a moment he smiled proudly as confidence swept over him, followed by a feeling of hope that his friendship with Hannah wasn't dashed. Whilst The Watchers were growing darker, The Gifted Ones were growing brighter. Hannah and Mini's imaginations were now fuelled by the new pure white light bestowed on them by The Spirits.

They were creating their own army as each character in the house began to come alive. The Spirits gift to Hannah and Mini had further strengthened their imaginations and in doing so had made the characters in the house become even more alive than ever before.

The markings on Pentheus gleamed as he sauntered his way around the house, purring whilst delivering his stately orders.

Parky's coat sparkled and his immense wings hung heavy off the shelf. He was lying down resting his head on his paws calmly watching events unfold.

Acting as a beacon, Nancy's torch had never shone so brightly.

She was the first to notice the Watchercrows and in her drawl anxiously said, "Oh I say, oh I say, they're coming!"

Hearing the warning, Hannah ran up the stairs towards the owl who was flapping insanely, then climbed off the stairs onto Parky's shelf, as she awkwardly peered through the square window in front of the chandelier. She could see not only the constellations but also the mass of black approaching; the crow army.

Feeling her heart pounding she looked down towards Parky.

"I will have to face them soon, Hannah," he said, looking up at her.

"Not yet, I have a plan," she replied calmly.

Within seconds of her reply, the oils of the moon painting hanging above the shelf began bubbling, causing the whole moon to surface from the canvas. It seamlessly passed through the square window rising into the night sky. As it ascended it grew to an immense size alongside the constellations, which shone vividly.

Hannah's plan had worked as even more Watchercrows began to drop away in fear, whilst others were converted back to being Gifted.

Enraged, Victor responded by spewing out a dark grey smokey light which projected towards the constellations. Other Watchercrows were doing the same and ribbons of grey fumes began to choke the air.

Their light carried a crushing force, but nothing could extinguish a Gift from The Great Star of the Cosmos and their efforts were in vain.

"It's time, Hannah," Parky said, as he slowly rose up on all fours. A law unto himself and magical even beyond Hannah's imagination, Parky mysteriously began to fulfil not only Hannah's but also his own destiny.

He would fly south to the Bretalina mountain range towards The Mindful Watchers, in the hope of diverting the Watchercrows from Mini's. They would be unable to resist being drawn to him.

Standing in the hallway, Parky glanced over his shoulder. Time in Hannah's imaginative world stood still. The beautiful bedlam in full swing had now paused, making his heart heavy.

Parky watched as he had done so many times before.

The owl flapping insanely at the top of the stairs, now infinitely still.

Wallis and Bertie, who had stepped out of their frames to dance on the stairs, were now paused in an embrace like statues.

Pentheus, his old friend, with paw raised, was pointing a claw and doing what he did best, orchestrating events.

Nancy the lamp was bent over carrying the heavy burden of her torch, keeping a loyal lookout.

Then, catching a glimpse at the painting of the young, beautiful and valiant Mini, time snapped back.

Magically, the high, white, double vaulted doors flung open.

Lowering and shaking his head, then pointing his chin upwards, Parky tucked in his beautiful white lustrous wings in preparation for flight and within seconds he was airborne.

Victor watched as a horde of Watchercrows were magnetically drawn into Parky's flightpath. An overriding desire by them to produce the same dark grey crushing force that had been used to try to expel the constellations, was overwhelming.

Taking control back over the horde Victor tactically led them towards the direction of Parky and once again called upon The Great Gifted Nickolous, emitting an almighty squawk that shook the sky. The sound was so piercing that the sky rumbled and the vibrations created sent shock waves rippling through the air, causing the crow army to be blown off course.

Tom hung on tightly to the unicorn's mane as they were both tossed up into the air. Having had sight of Parky amidst the disturbance he was now nowhere to be seen.

In the distance The Great Star of the Cosmos shone brightly above the mountain range, its long narrow rays appearing to touch the mountain summit.

The air had now settled and as the crow army drew closer to the range the most magnificent sight appeared to all present. It was Parky, having grown at least twenty times larger, majestically rising over the summit.

The Star's rays shone directly upon his copper coloured coat, and his pure white wings with their enormous wingspan clapped the air in stately fashion. His eyes were placid and his composition poised.

As the crow army advanced towards his splendour the earth began to quake, the mountains rumbled and from the broken ground a multitude of crows, that had been summoned by The Great Gifted Nickolous, burst forth from the depths of the earth.

Flying towards Parky the sound of flapping feathers and cracking rock resonated across the plains. Thousands of Watchercrows expelled their dark evil force, trying to extinguish Parky from The Gifted Ones' imaginations.

Black feathers smothered his body and in no time the dark light drained his spirit away.

Tom lowered his head in disbelief as he watched Parky's body become limp. Unable to control his grief, tears fell upon the unicorn's mane, turning the colour of the unicorn from black to white. Many of the Watchercrows that were pecking at Parky suddenly stopped, diverting their attention towards Tom and the unicorn.

Now with pure white hair and feathers it reared mid-air and, galloping through the sky, bounded towards Mini's to aid The Gifted Ones.

Tom, looking back, saw thousands of beaks, led by Victor carrying Parky through the air, dangling like a drowned rat suspended by its shoulders.

It was just as Belinda the portrait had foretold.

'It was Parky, he had grown at least twenty times larger and majestically rose over the summit.'

CHAPTER FOURTEEN

BATTLE OF MINDS

Death consumed the sky as Parky's lifeless body was being hauled by the crows through the still, silent air.

Nancy the lamp was the first to witness the savage scene. Tearily, in a shaky voice she said,

"Oh Miss Hannah, Oh Miss Hannah," wobbling nervously, tilting, she continued to peer through the blinds.

"Speak up woman, what is it, what do you see?" Pentheus questioned impatiently, clambering up onto Parky's shelf to look himself.

Standing confidently at the foot of the stairs, Hannah bore the pure white light which the Spirts had granted her. Within that extraordinary imagination Mini had become her younger self and was cutting through the air with her sword, like a samurai honing their skills ready for battle.

Duchess the lion had scrambled clumsily up the stairs to follow

Pentheus and upon reaching the top of the stairs herself, Hannah let out an enormous agonising shriek.

"Mini!" she cried out. Mini ran up the stairs.

Dropping her sword in utter disbelief, she froze and stood with the others in sorry awe.

Shocked, she put her hands over her mouth as tears streamed uncontrollably down her face. It was as though a knife had pierced her heart as she watched the body of the panther she loved so dearly being humiliated.

Turning to Hannah she wrapped her arms tightly around her. The Spirits, fully aware of the situation, moved over to where Mini and Hannah were and floated above their heads to allow their minds space to absorb the impending shock.

Looking up at the face of her Grandmother on the body of the young Mini, Hannah said sternly, as her bottom lip quivered,

"Mini, if we want to win this war, we have to fight now." With those few words the house went into full attack.

The ferocious Watchercrows, led by Victor had crushed Parky's spirit and dumped his body. As before some of them, consumed by fear had dropped away, whilst others, withdrawing from the murder were converted back to being Gifted Ones.

Those remaining began to fill Mini's house, whilst Victor was perched on the roof squawking at the moon and constellations.

Tom and the unicorn, ahead of the Watchercrows, had already arrived at Mini's and wasting no time came to the defence of The Gifted Ones.

Tom felt his own Gift was being restored and as his energy rose felt closer than ever before to Hannah, as the two of them began to work in unison.

Outside the house the unicorn was batting away the multitude of crows, flying mid-air with its enormous white wings, like a tennis player hitting balls on a court, as they continued to invade Mini's home.

Tom immediately went in search of Hannah. The light from him shone brighter than ever before because he finally trusted and fully believed in his Gift.

Finding Hannah's light amidst the black feathers dominating the house, he took her by the hand and his eyes lit up at the sight of her face. She was happy to see him but was still clearly disgruntled and snatched her hand away.

"Hannah, let's use our Gifts together to defend our friends," and once again finding himself at her mercy, he pleaded in desperation, "Please."

His voice was hoarse, and Hannah could see the urgency in his eyes. She didn't have a choice, there was no time to waste, the house was beginning to crumble under The Watchers.

"Go with him, Hannah," Mini implored, slicing her sword through the air with a vengeance, dicing crows to pieces as they attacked.

Within seconds both Tom and Hannah's imaginations had escalated, finding themselves as hawk and raven again. Now together, each stood bold in their battle armour. Tom, zealous as a hawk; his faith had made his stature grow in confidence. His eyes, while soft and dark, were razor sharp surveying the hallway.

Zoning in on Nancy the lamp, now in trouble, he screeched to Hannah to join him. Nancy was surrounded by the crows and was suffocating under their dark forces. Tom aggressively nudged his way in with his hooked beak.

Realising under his camouflage that he wasn't a Watcher, one of the crows expelled its dark grey force but Tom's valour and light knocked it away.

Alas though, they were too late for some, and the crows had zapped Nancy out of Hannah's imagination forever.

Melting like a candlestick, she disintegrated onto the floor and was gone.

Hannah flew over to Pentheus who was also holding on for dear life. He recognised her with his sad yet still courageous eyes. He had been torn to shreds and was losing the strength to fight.

Growing in size, Hannah managed to cover his entire body from head to tail, protecting him from the constant pecking and crushing force. However, what she didn't know was that Victor, perched on the roof, had only moments before directly hit Pentheus with his own powerful force, as it had penetrated through the roof.

"Hannah my dear," Pentheus said, with his last heavy, dying breaths. "It's been a pleasure," then closing his eyes he vanished from Hannah's imagination forever.

Lowering her raven head she felt a blanket of sorrow wash over her.

Looking up with a mixture of anguish and anger she saw Victor through a small hole in the roof that he'd cut out with his hooked beak. There he perched, with his raven head tilted backwards, giving out another almighty squawk, piercing the night air and causing the house to shake.

More victims became apparent. Wallis and Bertie, who had acted as loyal decoys by confusing and diverting the Watchercrows, had vanished. The frames where they once were, were now empty.

The owl had also disappeared. Crushed and stolen from Hannah's beautiful mind.

The Spirits came out in force. They mysteriously multiplied and their translucent tails could be seen darting amongst the black feathers. Then they performed the most miraculous conversion.

Giggling, they came face to face with almost every Watchercrow, mirroring them, revealing the people they used to be when they believed and were Mindfully Gifted. Some were instantly converted into their former Gifted selves. Their faith and Gift restored, they glowed with happiness.

The Spirits, knowing that their work was accomplished, returned to The Great Star of the Cosmos, their tails lighting up the sky as they returned home.

Some Watchercrows that had left the main murder within the house had gathered around Victor on the roof.

Hannah, no longer a raven and Mini, looking like her Grandmother, again both skilfully coordinated their imaginations to bring the burning sun painting to life, knowing that now was the right time.

Like moths to a flame the crows couldn't resist the Mindful energy that had been created and they were instantly extinguished by its sprouting flames.

Tom, now recognisable as himself astride his unicorn, could see Victor outside, retreating as the flames were enticing more and more Watchercrows.

Tom roared with authority, "Victor, not so quickly!" taunting him, as he cowardly fled the scene of destruction. Looking back at Tom, his crow eyes bore the softness Tom had briefly seen before, except this time they were edged with fear.

The Great Star of the Cosmos was shining brighter than ever; shining on those that shine.

Its rays were now brighter because The Watchers had, for now, almost been defeated.

As Victor flew away its pure white light, so blinding, overcame the darkness within him as he fell defeated to the ground.

'The unicorn was batting away the multitude of crows, flying mid-air with its enormous white wings.'

Chapter Fifteen

A Hope in New Beginnings

It had been a few days since The Watchers had cruelly dumped Parky's body. Now, it was a mystery to The Gifted Ones how he had returned; Parky's body lay in front of the high, white, double vaulted doors. Mini, Hannah and Tom knelt, lost in grief next to him with their heads hung low. Following the battle of minds Tom had visited Hannah every day.

Reaching to stroke his soft velvet ears, Hannah and the others came to the realisation that they weren't imagining anymore. Parky was in front of them as a real panther, except that now he was dead. Sobbing helplessly, Mini tried to console Hannah and Tom, wrapping her arms tightly around them both.

As Tom stared blankly at Parky he suddenly realised he had forgotten to return the Book of Spells to Hannah.

Feeling for it in his pocket, relief washed over him knowing that it was still there. Then looking over at Hannah he momentarily wondered what to do. He still felt he wanted to win her over, not only to apologise for letting her down, but also to impress her.

In that moment he finally understood his feelings and realised he was falling in love with her.

He reached for the tiny book again, and removing it from his pocket placed it in the palm of his hand and passed it over towards her.

"Er, I think you lost this," he said, coyly bowing his head as he presented it to her.

Sensing the strong connection between the two of them Mini stood up and took a few steps back.

Then taking a deep breath in with a tiny thread of hope, he peered up at Hannah, and taking both of her hands into his, encasing the Book of Spells, said,

"Please forgive me."

His apology was so sincere and heartfelt that it left Hannah with an overwhelming tickling feeling in her tummy that she'd never felt before. It stirred a similar energy inside her to that of when her imagination came to life, except in a different way.

Keeping the Book of Spells firmly in her hand she spontaneously flung her arms around his neck and they embraced. Hannah felt her heart beating fast and feeling flushed she pulled back, glancing down in a blush. They were falling in love with each other.

Just then the Book of Spells began twitching in her hand, and looking down she noticed the golden clasp glistening, beckoning her to open it. She looked at Tom in surprise and he nodded his approval to look inside.

Their worlds had collided. Both now shared mutual affection and trust for each other. The golden clasp, shining bright like The Great Star itself was an important part of Doodle's gift signifying that even in difficult times, when you place your trust in the Star all things can be held together.

She remembered what Mrs Doodle had said, that the book could only be used in life or death circumstances.

Slowly, opening the clasp, she read aloud the message written in ink on the tiny papyrus pages,

If forgiveness is accepted, eternal life will be granted to the one who herein lies sleeping.

Hannah, having already forgiven Tom with all her heart, noticed that Parky was miraculously beginning to stir. True to the tiny book.

An aura surrounded him, and his coat began to sparkle and twinkle, just as it had before, and a light seemed to emanate from within.

Tom and Hannah leant back, slightly fearful at first but then curiously edged forwards.

As Parky's eyes began to open Hannah could see her own reflection in them. His fear, apprehension and sadness had gone, replaced instead with love, peace and happiness. Hannah threw herself onto him wrapping her arms around his neck,

"Oh Parky, you're alive!" she exclaimed, with tears of joy.

He smiled at her and moving his body again slowly shook himself, knocking Hannah backwards, toppling onto Tom's lap.

Smiling up at Tom she nuzzled into his chest and he looked down, lightly kissing her forehead.

Parky strolled over to Mini, his faithful friend of old and rubbed his head against hers.

"I never doubted you, old friend," she said, with a tear in her eye whilst rubbing his head.

It was a new beginning for all. Parky had been granted eternal life, just as the Book of Spells had said, irrespective of Hannah's imagination.

Parky decided to stay on the shelf at Mini's, just as he always had and where he belonged.

As for Hannah and Tom it was The Great Star of the Cosmos that had coordinated their paths.

Ultimately though, it was their own belief, faith and love in their Mindful Gift, as well as each other, that fulfilled not only their destinies but Parky's as well.

Peace reigned at Mini's as Hannah enjoyed the last few days with her and Tom.

During this time and aware of her forthcoming departure, Mini continued with her obligation to further prepare Hannah about what lay ahead for her on the return home to Ashby-by-the-Sea. She once again felt that now was the opportune moment to explain to her Granddaughter about her deceased Grandfather.

In a tearful parting, Tom promised he would correspond regularly with Hannah and somehow visit her in England. Toms life had begun again, and he needed to work out how it would progress.

The Watchers were in disarray since the battle and although now secure in himself, Tom wondered how it would all work out. Many people from within his own and surrounding neighbourhood had had their lives drastically changed and in some cases for the better.

On Hannah's very last night at Mini's, after what had been the summer of a lifetime, the stars above the house shone brighter than ever before.

As Hannah passed Parky on the stairs, just as she had done on her very first night, she paused, taking in his magnificent splendour, and smiling back at her he winked and said,

"Goodnight Hannah," in his deep husky tone, then curled up on the shelf.

Sitting at the top of the stairs smiling proudly whilst watching their exchange was Mini. Here she thought would be the perfect place to talk with Hannah with Parky listening on.

"Your Grandfather was a suave man, suited and booted, always impeccably dressed. A true gentleman. He was born in England, like you."

Mini gazed up at the chandelier wistfully, reminiscing. A tear came to her eye as she wrapped an arm tightly around her. She was about to embark on another emotional journey as she proceeded to share once again, her past.

Hunter Lang was 28 when he met Mini in America.

Tall and lean, with platinum blond hair, which was accentuated by his pale blue eyes, hidden behind fashionable black glasses accompanied by a neat salt and pepper moustache. He was well-groomed and the epitome of old Hollywood glamour.

His move to America as a young ambitious debonair man, came from a career opportunity which he grasped wholeheartedly, as he embraced the new world.

His parents were both Naturals and had good connections in the transatlantic financial industry, in which he worked. Already knowing Bertie and Wallis enabled him to take up their kind offer of lodging with them in America. It came at the right time, as Victor had left home unexpectedly and rarely kept in contact and alas, Doodle had never returned from the circus.

His meeting with Mini recently returned home from the circus, was therefore inevitable and their love quickly grew.

It was Hunter's disastrous chance meeting one day with Victor where it all went horribly wrong and he didn't confide in Mini about it for many years to come.

Watchers tended to look after their own in business, caring for most of the home and business needs by the approved Watcher providers.

Occasionally, however, lines with The Gifted would become blurred, and even more so with Naturals, because The Gifted were only to acutely aware of their 'Watching' habits.

Hunter's company had been having financial dealings with

The Spectacle council. After being lured into a series of meetings, Victor, out of spite and jealously, knowing exactly who Hunter was, seized the opportunity to vengefully pounce and brainwash him, in order to take control.

Hunters ambitious nature would be a contributing factor leading to his demise.

He battled the Mindful Watchers for the rest of his life, torn between good and bad.

In Mini, he saw a pure innocence, similar to that which drew Tom to Hannah. A move back home to England for Hunter with his new bride Mini, was, he thought his only hope of escape.

Victor, vindictively in his last meeting with Hunter reminded him that there was no escape from The Watchers and that the founding fathers were world-wide.

'He'll be waiting for you at the castle.' Were his last haunting remarks.

In their new home-town of Ashby-by-the-Sea, Hunter provided meticulously for Mini as they settled into their new life.

Having lived in the same house where Hannah now lived, Mini went on to tell her that in her early married days, an owl's hoot from the Ash tree across the street at night, would comfort her homesickness at night.

On their first wedding anniversary Hunter had bought Mini a wooden sculpture of an owl with the words inscribed '*Never leave me in the dark.*' How apt those words would become.

"That's the very same owl there." Mini said, pointing to it at the top of the staircase."

Hannah now understood its significance as Mini's imaginary friend and now herself.

"Hannah, I have to warn you," Mini said most seriously, whilst looking directly at her.

"There are Watchers in Ashby-by-the-Sea."

"Your Grandfather eventually confided in me that he had become a Watcher, but of course, I already knew." Mini sighed.

Parky who was listening intently slowly lowered his head onto his paws.

"He tried desperately hard to resist the temptation and frequented The Flushing Meadows often."

"What are they?" Hannah asked, feeling as though she were being drawn back to the beginning of her summer, overawed by the intensity of the information being given.

Mini proceeded to explain how Watchers, as Watchercrows went to these meadows in the hope of flushing out dark forces, in the expectation of conversion. As a way of attracting The Great Stars attention they would perform a series of tumbles, ascending at speed then falling. Only if they truly believed and wanted to be converted from the darkness could the process occur.

"As you know, Watchers don't take kindly to betrayal, so the cleansing process is highly forbidden and comes at a huge risk." Mini explained.

"There's actually a Flushing Meadow not far from where you live on the outskirts of a small town called Pocklington. I'm sure you'd know it, it's actually within The Watchers neighbourhood.

They exist up in the Bretalina Mountains too. Usually they're an area of rough green or dry uninhabited pastureland.

A couple of things began to dawn upon Hannah, firstly was this why Tom perhaps rode his motorbike there, because the mountains had a Flushing Meadow and also was it why her parents had always forbidden her from playing in Pocklington.

In Hunter's final days whilst Mini was heavily pregnant with Belinda, he shared with her the persistent rumour within Watchers circles of the alleged remains of The Great Gifted Nickolous in a European castle. The said castle being the one in Ashby-by-the-Sea.

Mini, tearfully, explained that it seemed Hunter had been severely tormented by The Watchers and that Victor's prophecy about the castle was disturbingly accurate. Ashby Castle was indeed the final resting place for The Great Gifted Nickolous as well as the breeding place to a new deadly species of Watcher.

Hunter had been found dead in the castle grounds, wearing a dark suit; his dress had gradually darkened over the years.

Lying flat on the ground, facing upwards and looking petrified, in one hand were his shattered glasses and in the other a few silver coins.

Parky lifted his head up, his ears held tightly back as he listened to Hunter's demise. He watched as Hannah hugged her Grand-mother tightly. He could sense that she not only felt sad for Mini but also for the Grandfather she never knew. Hannah's feelings soon moved to anxiety with thoughts of what lay ahead at home, accompanied by the added fear of a new breed of Watcher.

Mini could see by her expression that all the information was racing around in her mind and as always, she tactfully interceded.

"I can tell you what I know. Remember the light will overcome the darkness and The Star will provide."

With those reassuring words they both fidgeted to sit more comfortably up against the wall of the stairs, looking directly at Parky. Mini began to tell her all that Hunter had confided in her immediately before his death.

Mini described how in the castle crypt, narrow steps lead down to where The Great Gifted Nickolous was laid in a copper casket. Mourner Watchers were believed to throw tear filled crow feathers down the steps to land upon it.

Over the centuries the crypt had filled with water and the burial ground was submerged by an underground stream. Early Watcher-guards had extracted what relics they could, as other smaller underground waterways were connected. The myth about Watchergaurds laying their eggs in the crypt was true. A new breed of Watcher was born. Flying fish. A winged creature with the body of a lizard and face and beak of a crow.

Hannah looked at Mini in horror.

"So now you will have to be even more skilful in your continued quest against The Watchers."

Putting both arms around her, she buried her head into her Grandmothers chest taking in that smell of her old-fashioned sweet fragrance once again. She'd miss her terribly and felt so fortunate that she'd had time to seal an unbreakable bond with her. She then felt an agonising pain at the prospect of what lay ahead and the thought of leaving Parky.

In that moment she looked up to Parky and he winked at her in the same way Mini had. She knew, returning a tiny smile back, that he was cemented in her mind forever and his spirit lived on. He would help her on her continued journey.

Sinking into the bed sheets and closing her extremely weary eyes that night, Hannah diverted her thoughts to that of Tom and pictured him on his motorbike. It was a welcome respite from the intensity of the evening's conversations. The corners of her mouth lifted as she proudly thought of the journey he had shared with her. She was truly smitten with him and she wondered what her parents and Amelia would think of him when he would eventually visit.

She had an overriding feeling that she'd need him when she returned home and she was right.

As it would happen, that night Belinda the portrait visited her in a dream with her own disturbing prophecy. Emerging from the portrait, she appeared in her usual attire, but her face was that of Hannah's mother. In the background there stood a medieval castle in ruins with a huge great tower, surrounded by a wide ditch, the sunken land resembling a dried-up moat. There seemed to be much activity in and around it, but her mother's unsettled face was hiding the chaos.

"Hannah, you must come home quickly darling, it's Amelia," she said anxiously.

The dream ended abruptly. Sitting bolt upright in a cold sweat, Hannah reiterated the words to herself. Everything Mini had told her came flooding back. She lay in the darkness feeling perplexed and frightened.

Leaning over to the night stand she switched the lamp on. Gaining composure, she could see in the soft night light there sat a small box, with an oversized red satin bow wrapped tightly around it. A pert brown paper tag read,

Always together in heart, Wink, Mini x

Hannah opened the box. It was a necklace with a pendant of a panther.

Without hesitation she put it on, and a familiar warmth caressed her entire body and the pendant glowed.

Placing her hand on the pendant she closed her eyes and sighed, feeling momentarily secure. It would become her 'Parky pendant'. It seemed Mini, like The Great Star, never ceased to provide.

Her mind, though, anxiously soon drifted yet again, and she had an overwhelming fear that The Watchers would be waiting for her in Ashby-by-the-Sea.

And so, as one tale ends another shall begin.

And I, The Great Star of the Cosmos, shall continue to share The Panther Tales with you and shine on those that shine.

For where there is good, there is always evil.

'A portrait of a stylish, blonde haired lady, dressed in a bright green sweater, with beautiful red fingernails.'

'It was a necklace with a pendant of a panther.'

About the Author

Daniella Marie Rushton is British, born 1973. Wife to Nicholas and Mother to Bertie.

Over the course of several summers whilst vacationing with her family, in the delightful desert sun of the Coachella valley, California, she formulated the concept of The Panther Tales.

Her son, challenged her to channel her renowned imagination into writing a book series. The Panther Tales was born and 'The Watchers and The Gifted Ones' is the first book of the series. After sharing her desire to create an imaginary world with an artist friend, a collaboration of creativity began with Zoe Potter who would become the illustrator.

Living a thoroughly creative life, Daniella busies herself with not only the ongoing series of The Panther Tales, her dog Walter and her family and friends. She is also an advocate in the Christian faith, believing in oneself, finding and using ones 'Gifts' in life.

Follow her on:

Instagram, Twitter or Facebook @thepanthertales

All artwork is available for purchase as prints. For more information please email thepanthertales@gmail.com

The panther on the shelf, the inspiration behind, *The Panther Tales*.

Made in the USA
Las Vegas, NV
29 April 2021